Crackers

Crackers

an anthology

Edited by Debz Hobbs-Wyatt and Gill James

Bridge House

British Library Cataloguing in Publication Data

A Record of this Publication is available from the British
Library

ISBN 978-1-907335-59-4

This edition published 2018 by Bridge House Publishing
Manchester, England

All Bridge House books are published on paper derived
from sustainable resources.

Contents

Introduction 7

Angel's Wing 8
   Alyson Faye

Believing Lies 16
   Stephen Faulkner

Supermarket Sweetheart 26
   Jennie E. Owen

No Fool like an Old Fool? 30
   M Bulleyment

Crackers the Clown 46
   Anne Wilson

Cracks in the Mirror 54
   Sally Angell

In Plain Sight 64
   Kay Middlemiss

Dress Form 69
   Christopher Bowles

Eton Mess 84
   Merlin Ward

Firecracker 90
   Elizabeth Cox

Horseflesh 97
   Adrian Naylor

Julia's Crackers 116
   G. Norman Lippert

Rescue Me, Saving You 127
  Linda Flynn

Sheep Be Damned 132
  Dianne Stadhams

Snap 138
  Karen Kendrick

Snow 150
  Ian Inglis

The Annual General Meeting of the East Kent Macumba
Society 160
  Michele Sheldon

The Bogeyman 170
  Steve Wade

The Flaw 181
  Stuart Larner

The mePhone 185
  Boris Glikman

Timothy and Pandora's Box 190
  Dawn Knox

Up in Smoke 207
  Paula R C Readman

Very Little Helps 220
  Clare Weze

Years of Eclipse 228
  L F Roth

Index of Authors 240

Introduction

Every year we pick a very vaguely Christmas-related theme for our annual anthology. Then we invite our writers to subvert it. In this collection, they've certainly done that to the extent that we almost had a picture of cream crackers for the cover. As you can see, though, in the end we went for firecrackers.

This collection has pieces by some of our regulars, some by new writers we picked up through the Waterloo Festival, and some by people we've never met before.

There was a very high standard in the submissions this year. All the ones we didn't select would surely find a home somewhere and indeed would be welcome on CaféLit. – http://cafelit.co.uk/index.php/submission-guidelines-2

The editing was easy this time. Writers are getting a real sense of what we're about and are very professional as well. There was little to do.

So here we have it: our collection of "crackers". Cracking good stories in any case. It's that time of year again and here we do concede to Christmas. Whatever your feelings about the season, those dark evenings when it's cold outside represent the ideal time to snuggle down with a good book.

So, that's what we're inviting you to do. We hope you enjoy our little collection. It would be great too if you would write us a review for Amazon, Goodreads, or indeed anywhere else you can think of. Reviews help writers and publishers.

Happy reading.

Gill James

Angel's Wing

Alyson Faye

Running for the school bus with Monday morning hair and bad breath, I trip and fall, skinning my knees. I watch the bus dwindle in the distance. Weak winter sunlight glints on something silver under the privet hedge.

Probably chewing gum foil, I think but intrigued I crawl under the twigs to grab it.

Above me, a stone angel looms, feet earthed firmly to the gravestone slab; one of many in St Peter's Churchyard. "Ma's local" as me and Dad like to joke. Mum doesn't laugh with us though.

The silver stuff isn't foil. Instead my fingers touch soft gauze; the sunlight refracting off the woven silver threads. It is a beautiful piece of fabric. I imagine fairies weaving it on tiny looms.

"All dreams you are. No common sense," Mum's always saying.

A deep voice startles me, "That's a piece of 'Angel's Wing' you've got there, love."

It is as if the stone angel has spoken. I jerk upright. Startled and wide-eyed. It's only Bob, the church caretaker and handyman. He is perched on the edge of the angel's tomb, eating his sandwiches. Tuna, by the smell wafting over the wall.

"What?" I gawp at him.

"I've got a box full of that Angel's Wing. Always finding it in the graveyard." Bob keeps munching, making clacking sounds. False teeth, I guess by how hard his jaw is working.

I give up on the notion of school for the day, for this conversation is more interesting than double physics. I haul myself over the wall and join Bob on his perch. I hand him the gossamer light lace. He holds it. Reverently. His head bowed.

"That's not silver thread. That's their veins. What carries their power."

He must see disbelief smeared across my features. "Not a believer then, lass?" He laughs, but not unkindly.

"Well how does it end up here?" I ask trying to be polite. Bob is about eighty and probably gaga, I think.

"Wherever they congregate. Where their images are recreated." Bob points at the stone angel towering above us. "See! They sheds the skin on their wings every few years so they can grow new ones."

"Like snakes?" I chirrup.

"Well there was a serpent in the Garden of Eden weren't there?" Bob asks. I try to follow his line of reasoning. But fail.

"So have you seen... er... an angel for real?"

"Nah – But I've been trying. All me life. On the look out. Keeping hoping."

Bob shoots me a sharp glance, which makes him look younger. "I know you don't believe me, lass. So let me show you summat."

He gently drapes the lacy Angel's Wing across my skinned knees. I feel a buzzy tingling warmth. Silver light shoots from the threads, winding around my knees like a glittery lasso. The tingling increases. My knees burn as if they are on fire. Then it's over. Vanished in a heartbeat. Looking down I see my knee caps are healed. No scratches, no blood. Grubby as normal. The Angel's Wing lies on the ground; grey and shabby looking. The glitter faded.

"See!" Bob sounds triumphant. "Better than the NHS init?"

I gape, awestruck. "You could sell this on eBay and make a fortune."

Bob frowns. "Nah, reckon the postal service would kill its power. It's tied to the church and the angel it comes from. Genetic divine link."

He says this with absolute authority. "Here, have my last tuna sandwich."

Bob holds out the white bread sandwich. I take it and nibble cautiously. I decide it's not the time to mention I am vegan.

"So who else knows about this?" I wave a hand at the surrounding graves and my knees.

"You and me, lass. Not the vicar that's for sure. Not him with his iPhone and 'Dial a Sermon' help line, rushing here and there in his Fiat. In my day vicars rode bicycles and wore trouser clips. Proper clergy they were."

The disdain in Bob's voice for the young jolly reverend, who always has a smile for everyone, is a surprise to me. I assumed he was universally loved by his flock. Mum's always saying he's 'innovative,' 'energetic' 'with great people skills' and rolling her eyes at Dad to imply that Dad is anything but.

I'm planning to tell her I did 'volunteer befriending' today using Bob as my designated senior person, to explain why I skipped school.

Perhaps I can persuade Bob to write a note? I ponder my options.

Bob shuffles closer and I edge away. He's harmless I reason. I can outrun him any day.

"I'll show you the ridges on their stone wings. You can count them. Like on trees." He creaks to his feet.

I follow him and walk over to a majestic Victorian stone angel which is hovering over a rectangular box tomb. Bob, showing surprising agility, pulls himself up onto the slab and then tugs me up after him. I stand nose to nose with the angel's navel. If it has one of course. Which it doesn't. Staring at the moss and tiny insects crawling over the stone, I wonder: do they tickle? Or perhaps angels are so divine they are beyond such basic discomforts?

"Here, rub your fingers on this spot." Bob guides my hand to the angel's right wing. It soars above us, lichen coloured. To my surprise I can feel circular ridges, a few centimetres apart. Regular and repeating. Bob is nodding, his eyes all shiny and bright. Like a squirrel showing me his cache of secret winter food.

"Sign of wing regrowth that is."

I'm not sure. It might be the work of a Victorian stonemason. Though I have to admit it's unusual. I suppose it could be true.

"It's on them all," he adds. "I've checked."

I stare at the tiers of stone angels surrounding us; small, medium and super-sized. There is a holy committee of them.

"They're watching us," Bob adds, quite calm.

I pull my hand away as if it's burned. This is an appalling thought.

"My favourite is this chap here." Bob points to an angel lolling as if he's drunk, in a neglected corner by the fence. "That's Bernard."

This is getting stranger and stranger. Bernard doesn't sound angelic to me.

"Do they all have names?"

"Course they do, luv. Well we do. So why wouldn't they?" Bob's logic, is as always, faultless.

A fresh voice breaks into our reveries. "Morning Bob and er er. What are you doing up there?"

It's the smiley vicar, although he's looking cross at the moment. He's glaring at us, whilst holding his iPhone in one hand. Bob and I exchange glances.

"Morning, Reverend," Bob replies and he drops down to the wet grass before turning courteously to help me.

"Aren't you Val's daughter?" the vicar asks, peering at me.

I nod. "Rebecca."

Bob stands as tall as his 5 foot 4 inches will allow. He's much shorter than the vicar but he's on his home turf. He also has the heavenly hordes on his side.

"I am assisting Re-bec-a with her homework assignment. Victorian Gothic graveyard architecture," he announces. I gape at him seriously impressed. He thinks fast for a senior. "She has some interesting questions which involve closer inspection of the stone work."

The vicar lingers uncertainly. His iPhone trills, signalling he is a busy important man who doesn't have time for a scruffy school girl and the caretaker.

"Well make sure you don't damage anything or leave any litter." He glares at me and then stalks off holding his iPhone as though it's made of gold.

"Idiot," Bob murmurs. I'm thinking of ruder words than that.

He should be supportive of my project. I am indignant, until I remember, a few seconds later, there is no project. It's all a fiction.

The sky is clouding over. Grey is the dominant colour around us. Graves, stones, gravel and the air itself. It's time to head off.

I've been here hours. I glance at my watch. "Have to go. Bye, Bob. It's been interesting."

"I'll give you some Angel's Wing to take home with yer, love."

Bob shuffles over to a tomb, ferrets around underneath in a gap and pulls out a battered metal tin, pre-World War

II by the look of it. "I keeps it in 'ere."

When he shyly lifts the tin lid, I expect shooting stars and silver lights to emerge but instead we both peer at a dusty tangled skein of cobwebby stuff. I must look disappointed because Bob gently squeezes my shoulder.

"It don't look much when it's resting, but it'll work alright, lass."

He wraps it in a tissue and we part company. I leave Bob resting against a cherub, smoking his pipe with his cap tipped at an angle.

He's the oldest cherub in the place. I think. smiling to myself.

At home Mum is fuming. School have rung, as has the smiley reverend. Both to tell on me. It turns out Mum's volunteered me for cleaning the church hall once a week as penance. I make out I'm mad, slam a few doors and do the whole stropped act but secretly I'm OK with it because it means I can chat with Bob.

The first time I turn up after school on Wednesday for my cleaning duty, Bob isn't around. "He's in hospital. Not sure what with," the vicar tells me then he wanders off texting.

I'm not impressed.

I eye roll behind his back.

Outside winter is clawing at the sky and the light. The graveyard is gloomy and untidy. It's already missing Bob's ministrations. To help, I pick up some litter and bag it. Then I head off in the direction of Bradfield Royal Infirmary. I'm carrying the Angel's Wing in my bag, since I daren't leave it at home. It would be too weird explaining it to Mum.

Bob is on Ward 14. He looks half his usual size, lying shrink wrapped in white sheets; like an aged larva. He smiles and props himself up when he sees me though.

"Hello, love. Good to see you."

Excitement bubbles in me. I bend down and whisper, "I've got the Angel's Wing with me, Bob. In my bag. We can fix you up and you'll be out of here in no time."

I scrabble in my rucksack, keeping an eye open for a nosey nurse and pull out the cobwebby tangle. It looks unimpressive, rather like spiders' webs' rejects.

Bob eyes it and then me. He smiles. "I don't think that'll work for what ails me, love. But I'm glad you're a believer. You've got to believe in a bit of magic to keep you young."

In my hand the skeins crumble into dust, dribbling through my fingers. "No!" I cry out. Heads turn.

"Limited shelf life, love," Bob explains. "Guess nothing lasts forever." He pats my hand.

"I'll find some more. I'll come back and cure you. I will. I promise." I'm close to tears.

"What are you talking about, love? I'll be out of here on crutches in a week. A few sessions of physio. and I'll be right as rain."

My mouth drops open. "You mean you're not er well…?"

Bob laughs, showing his tonsils. "Not yet, love. Not by a long chalk."

The ward sister asks me to leave at that point. She says I am 'a disruptive influence in the ward.' Just like me and school all over again.

On the way home I walk through Bob's graveyard, though it's nearly dark and I know I'll be late for tea. I lean against Bernard, our stone angel, and rub its wing.

"Ow!" I pull my fingertips away. I'd picked up a static buzz off the stone.

Looking upwards, the stone angel is a dark silhouette

with its wings limned against the sky. It might be the angle of my head or because I've forgotten to put my contact lenses in that morning, so everything's blurry, but I'm certain Bernard's wings flutter. I feel a breeze stroke my cheek and I am comforted.

About the author
Alyson lives in West Yorkshire with her family. She writes noir flash fiction, film articles, spooky short stories and Y.A. novels. Her debut flash fiction collection, *Badlands*, has been published by Chapeltown Books in January 2018. Her fiction appears online at zeroflash, the Horror Tree, Horror Scribes, Coffin Bell Journal, Siren's Call ezines and in print anthologies like Women in Horror Annual 2 and DeadCades. When she's not hammering away on the pc she enjoys swimming, singing, films and crafting.

Her blog is at www.alysonfayewordpress.wordpress.com

Believing Lies

Stephen Faulkner

It all began as a fluke, a big joke. That was all it was supposed to be. We never meant it to get so out of hand and go so far as it did, but now is not the time for explanations or apologies. It has been done and gone overboard and there is nothing left to do but feel a cold sense of remorse for the whole affair – and for Dessy – and even that does no good, just lies there in the pit of your gut like a stone.

It was all a lie and we, Dessy and I, were its perpetrators. It was just a goof, a huge practical joke filled with so many inherent minor pranks built into it. What eventually happened can be blamed on the realistic validity of what began as a well-structured, beautifully executed, bomb of a lie. It was a private game and, like all our previous games, Dessy's and mine, once it was worked up to its ultimate perfection, then we turned it loose on the unsuspecting victim.

Mind games, all just childish teasers meant to build up, then batter down the expectations and self-confidence of the mark like the time Dessy played the dumb ox in History II for the entire semester, mixing up Gaul with Rome, Rome with Greece and all their respective generals, heroes, gods and writers until there was such a jumble of intertwining bits of meaningless misinformation being thrown around and twisted apart that Mister Henson was resigned to give Dessy up for a complete dolt, only later forced to give my friend and co-conspirator an A on his final exam, though a substantially lower grade for the course itself because of the previous months of his asinine behaviour. But the look on the teacher's face – and I was in the class at the time – of complete bewilderment as he handed Dessy back his graded test paper, I could see my friend's smirking wink, telling me that it was all well worth the B-minus that he received for the course itself.

And then there was the dying gag; I was the key player in that one. So there I was, writhing on the floor of the dormitory hall, groaning as loudly as I could, complaining of pains shooting through the left side of my abdomen – a definite appendicitis, right? – and I was hauled away like a convulsive sack of meal by Jackley (old Jack-off to most of the guys in our dorm), our floor overseer, into his room. Hoisting me onto his bed, tucking me in under a landslide of blankets and sheets, he ran outside to the phone at the end of the hall to call the nurse's office. Dessy's job was to make sure that old Jack-off was kept busy out there, asking a tremendous number of questions concerning my condition, pulse, breathing and if there was a fever and stuff until the men arrived with the stretcher. Of course, I was long gone from under the bundle of scratchy blankets and, in my place was a gloriously stripped down Susan Ganton (good old Suzy Creamcheese, always game for a ripe joke), covering up demurely while screaming obscenities at the top of her lungs at Jackley for bringing a party into their private rendezvous. Jackley will never be the same after that one, I am sure.

And then there was the time… but that's it, you see: there *was* the time. And it's all in the past now; now there is only the unforgivable present.

And it all began as usual, with Dessy and me planning our next Big One. It started, as always, with the talking, talking, talking, arranging and rearranging the incidents, working it all into a slowly evolving, believable charade. This one was to be our *pièce de résistance*, our final word to dear old Denbury Hall. It was our senior year; the final semester was already waning and we wanted to leave one last killer psych-out for all the faculty and student body to remember us by. All the previous "projects" of ours, though each perfectly conceived and rendered, focused on only one mark at a time and the astonishment engendered was but momentary, registering, in most cases, in the face and discombobulation of just one person. This last one was to be our grand finale, encompassing the whole populace of the school (if it all worked out according to our elaborate plan) from lowly freshman up to Headmaster Pralender himself.

The idea was originally posited by Dessy – short for Desmond – and quickly denied as a possibility by me. Denied too quickly, though for, as the full meaning and wide breadth of scope of the thing began to penetrate my defences and tickle my rather jaded sense of humour, I became slowly enthralled with the notion until, finally, I found myself asking, "How do we begin?"

"Well, it has to start slow," said Dessy. "And I mean at a dead turtle's pace slow or else they'll know we're pulling another one of our foolers and so they'll just discount it out of hand before it even can get off the ground."

"So? What do you suggest for a starter?"

"Melanie Lane's End of School Year party."

"Start there? How?"

"Look, her parties are usually just talking affairs, right? No music or dancing and not enough to drink to make a fly woozy. Just a lot of kids sitting around, shooting the breeze."

"Yeah," I said. "But before the night's done everyone seems to have paired off and gone off to one of the bedrooms or are sprawled out together in pairs on the living room floor. I know: I got busy with my tongue, tickling Betsy Werthman's tonsils and my hand fooling around in her panties searching for the something for my finger to

18

diddle. Boy did she stop that from happening real quick!"

"Uh... yeh," Dessy said with a strange look on his face. "Anyway – back to the point now – we'll have to get the ball rolling on our plan before end of year the whoopee-making begins."

"All right. But how?"

"Talk," said Dessy and then considered for a moment before going on. "If the conversation is about the upcoming Highland game, I'll just insert a few quips on the dissection of flowers. People will become annoyed at the intrusion, try to steer the talk back to the game and how it will turn out but I'll persist and become louder, if necessary, and really insistent, giving off a portion of Doctor Bokrell's speech on the subject – quite an eloquent fellow, that guy, really – and then, when I've got them all wondering what the fuck is this all about, then I'll say something to the effect that Highland has a terrible defence and that we can't help but beat the pants off of them. With that, I'll finagle the conversation back onto its original course until no one will be aware that anything odd had ever happened."

"It sounds a little brash, though, doesn't it?" I asked. "I mean, they'll know for sure it's a joke right away and then that'll be the end of it."

"Yes, but they'll think that *that* is the joke. But they won't see the overall plan. I butt in and crap up a conversation at a party for a while, folks are amused but so what? Regular talk continues and that's that – right? But that *won't* be just that. These strange little lapses in my mental stability will begin to occur again and again with increasing frequency until it's a forgone conclusion to everyone on campus that I've gone completely off the deep end."

"And when the school shrink gets through with you," I glumly concluded. "And you confess that it was all just a big joke, he'll either put you – and me – under intensive observation to find out the reason why we pulled such an insane stunt or else have our degrees suspended and be sure we never get one from any school at all."

"Semester's only got another six weeks to go," Dessy reminded with a wickedly hard clap on my back. "By the time the full realization hits them that I'm crawling up and down walls, we'll both be back home, eating chocolate and smoking like chimneys as we surf the internet for summer jobs and bugging our folks' friends and associates for tips on where to get work."

Regretfully, I yielded to him. I saw the sheer simplicity of the scheme as its main advantage and which was the one thing that was sure to make the whole thing a wild success.

"I only wish we could see the faces of those suckers when the full impact hits them," I said, smiling at the growing attractiveness of the plan. Now, I only wish I had never seen those faces. The eyes are the worst, really. Sadness brimming, sorry thoughts coming to the surface like dead fish in a super-heated pool.

When they dragged Dessy away, screaming like an evangelist to the crowd (the only intelligible words I could glean from his ranting was "Wrong! All wrong! Not supposed to go like... All wrong! Fucked up! Wrong!"), I wanted to show more than a sour face, a glum, sorry-Pal expression but that was all that I could manage, all that was left to me if I wasn't to be implicated in what had happened to my friend. No tears. Dessy and I had spent them all laughing.

"I know he was a good friend of yours," came an unexpected condolence from behind me. "I'm really sorry. It doesn't seem right, something like that happening to *him*. Such a great sense of humour..."

"Yeah, well," I said as I turned to go, hearing the faint

wail of the ambulance siren as it receded into the distance. "He brought it on himself."

Brought it on, I thought. Acted *too* well. Believed the lies we worked so hard to put across these past few weeks. A non-sequitur here, a bit of angry bullshit there, a whacked out soliloquy on some trumped up idea over there... But they were all lies – the madness, the gibberish, the behaviour – and he knew it. Lies. And he apparently began to take them to heart without my noticing, making them his own, making them a part of him, believing that they *were* part of him. But why? Were they *that* convincing to him? Was it simply because they *were* his own? Was that all that he had? I should have asked him a few weeks ago, even just a few days ago about it. If I had asked, put it to him, then it might have been enough to allay...

But, now, no use. No asking. Dessy won't tell, maybe just *can't* tell. I don't know. I don't even know if *he* knows. Whatever the case, he isn't saying, so caught up in his own world, his own web of lies. And now he's out of it, seemingly for good.

And still, I wonder. Still, the speculation, worrying through all the whys and what-ifs. Trying to figure out where it all went wrong, trying to make sense of it all.

But all still to no avail.

...all wrong. We missed something some little nuance or something in me that we didn't see that crapped it all up, Pal. You only believed in the outcome the shining faces gone sour with a madman babbling on about and about and about letting his guts show too well and we thought that that would be it but we didn't see past their gullibility to my own homegrown laughter up the sleeve rolling out of me and down the moonlit path panting like old seaweed on the pebbled shore. Do you see the pebbles, Pal? There was one that I stumbled over and you saw me do it because the pebble, bouncing and chuckling merrily as I hit the ground eating the pavement – that pebble was you! And there was me not knowing and thinking that it was just another phase of the game that took so much to plan and so little to unhinge and fall away like water from a gaping jaw.

The pebble, yes, that was it or maybe it was further back but let me think for acting crazy with all the non-sequiturs blows the sequence away across mellow plains into hairy caves past creamy thighs and if you feel my thigh you gonna get me high like when the paregoric soaked joint was passed around and it lifted us and I wanted to be lifted and to lift you, Pal, but it was in the way and we didn't see it 'til I tripped along with it over it into the crazy plain yes I know that I am though there's nothing to be done but let them drag me kicking trying to tell you it was all a waste from the start, all wrong and something else like knowing I was nutty to the end and playing the part so well so well to the very hilt all the time.

And I wanted to let you know that it was me there from the very first, Pal, friend, bosomchum, but it took that last pebble and it was so much more than the make believe than the believing and the make believe like so many others we have pulled – straight A student flunks out or makes good or the appendicitis sexpot scandal watching Jackoff creaming in his drawers at the sight of Creamcheese in the buff bawling dead serious about a party in the room and a tête-à-tête that surely could never have happened between them for you know she was someone else's troth though she would never say who it was only flash the ring and a juicy piece of titty smelling of lavender I got so close wanting to grab and fondle it or lay my tongue out to taste that cosy looking little nipple and then came an "Ah-ah! Mustn't, mustn't," she said with a finger wagged under my nose. "Or else my boyfriend will kill you if I tell." She was a luscious tart she was and I hated her or thought so when we began talking the way that you and I did so often, Pal, and got onto subjective topics and about how she felt about this and that and the other thing perhaps so there was no great gargantuan of a beau in the bushes waiting to geld me and she was sorry that she teased us so and stayed my active hand and eye so coarsely but that was her way to feel out and stay clean but she is no longer no longer and we lay ourselves out crispy clean on the empty floor with her leg draped pillowsoft and white over my hip and we did so on two successive Saturdays, one out of mutuality of desire but on the second when her talk ran comparisons from my first Saturday to your first Wednesday I pushed you right out of her head by sheer pneumatic force until sore and exhausted she swore and I believe her that you, Pal chum confidential buddy o' mine were gone from body and mind and that you would remain so forever more as long as I…

And so don't tell me otherwise because after that second time I never gave you an even chance to see, smell or touch that which I lay claim to night after night and she said so and I believe her but still stalk the back reaches when I can, worrying that your shower room maleness had penetrated farther than I could ever and so I kept you away and kept us laughing at the poor souls in their makeshift concern over our unwieldy charms and foolers not seeing until too late yes too late the seeing though I sensed it out there that one overbearing stumbling block of a sandy coloured pebble out there to get me and all you need is just one and everyone gets his not always like I got mine putting on the act, wrenching along at an accelerating pace for a goof a joke a lie and a fall I know it was like that an interrupted walk hand in hand on the beach face down in the water and we made believe that it was just part of the at the act though that was getting the best of me. I like it though it was all a lie all flaky bits thrown off like confetti from Santa's bag, toys and whistlers and the Highland game with mutilated flowers at my feet, growing with every additional quip that no one cared or dared to see it come from the deep heart and gut not even you, you the co-conspirator and confidante on the sidelines the coach couldn't grasp the wailing titters as something real something terribly real for you it was only a joke an extension of the lie but to me a whine a cry and need for a fallback and to let them all in on the shady doings though I couldn't tell you but for a simpering admission that it was going only *too* well as planned. And you loved that and made it sound as though the lie were just funfunfun and so egged me on to the end until Creamcheese Ganton seemed mere catpiss and childish masturbation in comparison as I threw out the whole length until it snapped to see you laugh hear your face crinkle and grow apples on your cheeks in joy at their unnerved consternations until the end fell away like a misty trap door under my wavering balance and you laughed as I knew you would and I went still further falling loving your face so full of slap happy mirth that I never wanted it to end, my pebble on the shore, yes *you*, Pal, my old bosom buddy in so many foolish prank-filled 'mesters, you are my rising faithful star for whom the end was met and the bottom reached – all for you, your open faced spirit of jovial absurdity. Yes, you, you, all for you.

For you, my pebble, just you.

Now come and lend Dessy a boosting, sour faced hand and get me the hell out of here. I don't like it here, where I am. It has long since ceased being charmingly good and jolly fun. Just a smile, yes, wan and good natured plus a word nicely chosen that it was all a lie – all a simple whispered lie and joke – harmless fun and I will believe you. Yes, I will. Didn't I before? Can't I do it again? Lie to myself that it was all a joke, a big, brash, go for broke joke and that I'm really not this fucked up ball of psychotic talker to myself kind of person?

That I'm really as sane as anyone you might meet on the street?

Can you tell me that now so that I can believe it? Even though it's still so very wrong wrong wrong all the words flying about in this tin drum I call my mind in voices only I can hear. Like now, here, in this empty, oh so empty room... I talk, but who is here to talk to but you, my sweet friend, my tripping pebble...? Can't you tell me that I'm sane so I can play the part, be that person? If you do, I know that I can pull it off and know to the bottomside of my being that I will. Yeah, really. So. Please, *please*, Pal, do it for me. Do it now. Just tell me, please, so I can be the me that you and I want me to be. I'll believe anything you tell me now, Pal. Really.

Just anything.

About the author
Stephen Faulkner is a native New Yorker, transplanted with his wife, Joyce, to Atlanta, Georgia. Steve is now semi-retired from his most recent job and is back to his true first love – writing. He has had the good fortune to get stories published in many publications including Aphelion Webzine, Unhinged and Hellfire Crossroads. He and Joyce and an ever-changing number of cats have a busy life working, volunteering at different non-profit organizations, and going to the theatre as often as they can find the time. His novel, *Aliana in Paradise*, has recently been published by World Castle Publishing and is available through Amazon.com and Barnesandnoble.com.

Supermarket Sweetheart

Jennie E. Owen

Tonight's the night as they say, and I'm just trying to, you know, to build up to it. I'm sat in my Fiesta outside the Asda, it's about 9.45pm and they'll be shutting soon, and I'm drumming my fingers on the steering wheel. I'm going to do it; I'm going to get her.

It's dark where I'm parked, far away from the lights and more importantly the security cameras. The green sign of the store is reflected in a hundred puddles. Half a dozen youths with hoods over their faces are hanging around the cash machine and the odd late night shopper passes out of the doors with a low swoosh. Not her though, I'll have to go in and get her.

Believe me I'm not a bad person. I hold down a job, have kids. Had kids. They're with their mum now, but I send money when I can. I've even got my own little flat. I'm a productive member of society me; I do my bit.

It started a few months ago. I've been by myself a couple of years; it gets lonely going back to the flat every night on my tod. Don't seem to have many friends, apart from Archie I guess when he's not plastered; but I've always preferred my own company. I come in on singles night, Tuesdays. Five meals for one, single serve anything, some beer, some vodka too if I feel flush. It's *unofficial* singles night of course, but we're all in here doing it. Mostly fat-thighed middle aged hags with varicose veins. They try to catch my eye sometimes, but I stare down at my white knuckles on the handle of the shopping trolley. Even the cashiers try it on with me, the girls *and* the boys.

Anyway, this one night I saw her and I just knew. She's

26

petit, dark, with these amazing brown eyes. She's called Beth; it says so on her name badge. She just seemed so friendly, stood there by Customer Services. I'd never seen her before, but she has a face you couldn't forget.

I started coming back more and more often. Not just Tuesdays, but two or three times a week. I'd sit in the café and watch her. Some of the others act like she isn't there at all, *bitches*. She'd be much better with me I thought. Then the idea wouldn't go away.

I was sat in the flat 2am, a vodka and red bull in one hand, remote in the other, The TV showing a vision of all the things I was missing in life. Adverts of happy couples and families eating yogurt together, or visiting the park; smiling those huge grins in every freaking ad break. I missed my kids, I even missed my ex. Then I started thinking about her, the Asda girl. Her sexy curves bulge in her uniform as she welcomes me into the store. Never judging, never turning me away. Her fringe hangs slightly over one eye, full red lips. God she's gorgeous. I can't tell you, you'd have to meet her in real life to understand.

I started to formulate a plan then and there, how I could bring her home. She'd be happy here, I could make her happy. We'd be blissful together, I knew we would.

So here I am, pulling on my gloves. I flex my fingers and the leather creaks. I pull the stocking over my head. The chocolate bar is in my pocket and the thick black tape is on the front passenger seat, just in case.

It's five to ten. I turn the radio down, leave the engine running and give one last tap on the steering wheel. I go. I'm legging it across the car park, there's no one around now, even the security guard has buggered off somewhere. The ground disappears under my feet, I'm slipping slightly on the wet tarmac. I'm at the entrance. I'm through the door. The smell of bread makes my stomach growl. Then she's there in front of me, that stunning smile on her face. The other Customer Service staff begin squealing like the fat little pigs they are, but it's too late. I throw her over my shoulder and she doesn't even struggle, like I'm her bleeding white knight or something. Someone is shouting for Security, to call the Police. I put my hand in my pocket and grab the king size Snickers, pointing it through my pocket to look like I'm tooled up. They drop to the floor. I can hear someone crying and I'm out.

I'm back at the car and pop the boot. Damn it, she's too tall to fit sideways; I slide her prone body around the other way and get the tape.

I'm back at the flat, in the car port. I realize I still have the stocking over my head. I pull it off and my hair is stuck to my face. I catch my reflection in the rear view mirror, yellow in the artificial light. My blue eyes are circled with whites that are mostly red.

I open the car door and inhale the cold air deeply.

I walk around to the back; the boot is hanging open, held secure with a criss-cross of tape. Beth's feet stick out the rear and it looks obscene, like a tongue lolling out of a mouth.

I rip the tape off and pull my sweetheart into my arms. I carry her like a bride up the steps to the door, three at a time. My palms are wet, my heart beating like a teenager. I finally have a grin like the yogurt family.

The key slides into the lock and we're inside. Her lips are cold as I kiss them. She's smiling. I stand her up by the window and check her over and I see there's a crease in her arm, it hangs strangely. The cardboard at her ankles is ripped but still she stands there, my Beth, a Goddess with light reflecting off her laminated skin.

About the author

Jennie E. Owen's writing has won competitions and has been widely published online, in literary journals and anthologies. She is a Lecturer of Creative Writing and lives in Mawdesley, Lancashire with her husband and three children.

No Fool like an Old Fool?

M Bulleyment

"Dreadful. Absolutely mind-numbingly dreadful! What was Plumcake thinking of? Even by his standards, that was dire. Rock around the clock? See you later, alligator? I'm not a child. It's my legs that don't work, not my brain."

"Calm down, Cora, for goodness sake. Now, you've got your chair stuck."

Magda patiently manoeuvred the wheelchair through the door and turned Cora around to face her.

"I'm sure Mr Plumrose thought that *The Fun Fifties* would be just that. The Memory Corner residents loved it."

"Precisely. It doesn't matter what you give them, they'll have forgotten it a minute later, but some of us will have recurring nightmares from that dreadful din. I can't wait until my son's back in the country and I can leave this cultural desert. You're the only person who keeps me sane in this place, Magda."

"You take everything so personally, Cora. Just relax. They can't please everyone here."

"My one fear in life has always been to end up in a place like this, where people's idea of fun is to entertain you with ancient pop music – that I loathed at the time – and pretend they're helping you relive happy, youthful memories. I mean... Oh, no."

"Now, what?"

"We've had *The Fighting Forties*; *The Fun Fifties* (smog and rationing?) so please tell me we're not having *The Swinging Sixties*. It'll be The Beatles, won't it and Memory Corner'll love every yellow-submarined note of it? Spare me."

"What a fuss you make about everything. What's wrong with The Beatles?"

"They were such frauds. They sang their 'compositions' into tape recorders; little bald-headed old men wrote them down and then a succession of little old men, harmonised, arranged and played on the recordings, until the 'Fab Four,' were good enough to play themselves. They were a packaged commodity, not musicians, and they didn't have to struggle through harmony exercises like the rest of us, either."

Cora finally paused for breath. "I'm sorry, Magda. Crabby old teacher takes her frustrations out on you. I'll shut up now, but please don't waste your time with those bed cushions, I'll only mess them up again."

"My father loved The Beatles," said Magda, abandoning the chaos strewn over Cora's bed. "The Beatles and Bartok."

"Interesting combination."

"Dad escaped Budapest during the '56 uprising. He ended up in London, where he met my mother. She's from Italy. I arrived four years later – Magda Maria – for both of them. London and The Beatles represented freedom with a capital 'F' for my dad, compared with what he'd left behind in Hungary. It's not just about playing instruments."

"I suppose looking at it like that, you have a point. I'm always opening my big mouth and putting my foot in it."

"I'm off, Cora. I'll be back with a cup of tea later. I'm guessing you'll not want to come down to the lounge and have tea with the 'musicians'."

Before Magda had reached the door, there was a knock on it. "Can I come in, Cora? It's Martin Plumrose."

"See you later alli – Cora." Magda laughed and slipped out, as Martin rolled in.

"Er… now, Cora, I'm not going to beat about the bush. Er… I know you've not integrated much with the other residents, er… but I've a favour to ask you."

31

"Integrated? I'm only here temporarily so what's the point, but ask away, ask away."

"Er... When the new wing of Rochester House opens on April 1st, we're planning a big event – er... ribbon-cutting by the mayor, press coverage and all that. Er... I would like you to head up a committee of residents, to help plan it."

"Why me? I might not be here by then."

"We'll cross that bridge when we come to it. Er... I know you've organised arts festivals and all that sort of thing and er... I saw you heading out of the lounge just now with your hands over your ears, er... so perhaps you can organise something more appropriate for this event."

"So you're really saying, 'if you don't' like it, organise something better yourself.' Well, why not."

It'll give me something to do, while I'm waiting to get out of here. Sorry, I know that sounds rude, but..."

"Don't apologise. Just give us a memorable event. Er... I'll get the committee ready to meet tomorrow. 11.00 in the conservatory?"

"Fine. I'll be there and I'll have a plan ready. Before you leave, would you mind switching on my CD player. There's a CD already in it. Real music with more than four chords."

Minutes later, as Cora was nodding in her chair, cushions and throws on her bed started sliding to the floor.

"What dirge disturbs my slumber, Corinna?"

"That dirge is by one of my favourite composers, Johnny. Henry Purcell. He wrote this not long after you'd died. It's exquisite. *When I am laid in earth,* sung by Dido, Queen of Carthage. Purcell died young, like you. His wife locked him out in the rain and cold, one night and he never recovered."

A balding head emerged from under the remaining cushions.

"The name I remember, but he accounted for little then."

"We had no one to match him for two hundred years."

"Like me?"

"Some of your poems were hardly to the taste of Queen Victoria and her subjects – unlike the royal circles you moved in."

"I believe my words 'cut and sparkled like diamonds'."

"That was earlier and I should never have told you that. Now listen, Johnny, you can help me. I'm organising an event on your birthday, when they open the new wing on the site of your old house. So, I thought a poetry recital might be a good idea. It might even restore your reputation a little."

"My reputation rests as it is."

"You know you don't mean that. I can get rid of that deathbed religious conversion nonsense for a start. I thought you could write something new for me."

"If the Muse comes."

"Don't be ridiculous, Johnny. You wrote most of your work when you were completely boozed up."

"My Muse was indeed alcohol, but apparitions cannot partake, so I am now in Hell."

"We both are, so we have to make the best of it."

The next morning, Magda breezed in for her morning round. "I hear you're to organise the Big Event."

"Wish me luck. I don't know who else is on the committee yet. I should've asked that before I said, yes."

"Colonel Drummond; Jilly Townsend; Frank Wren; Susan Belchamber…"

33

"You're joking. It's worse than I thought."

"You'll manage. Now let's get you up and at 'em."

The sun was already warming the conservatory when the committee assembled.

"Anything you need, er… just let me know. I'm confident that we'll organise a wonderful day."

Martin Plumrose smiled at the group gathered around the table, his chins wobbling in harmony.

"I've another meeting to attend but, er… I look forward to hearing what you've decided."

"We must have a band," said the colonel. "A marching band."

"No. No. No," Cora resisted thumping the table. "This has to be appropriate. A new wing of Rochester House. So let's think. Who was Rochester?"

"Not the foggiest idea," said the colonel. "I came here to be near my daughter, this place's history was hardly the point."

"What's this?" said Cora. "We have a pretty witty king/Whose word no man relies on/He never said a foolish thing/And never did a wise one."

"Charles the Second!" said Jilly.

"Yes. Made up on the spot by John Wilmot, 2nd Earl of Rochester, who was the King's Gentleman of the Bedchamber, a poet and a satirist. The remains of his old house – originally his father's hunting lodge – are somewhere underneath the new wing. So, let's celebrate the history of this place with poetry and music. Forget the usual band and food stalls. It's not the church fete.

Let's have something a little more sophisticated. Let's pick our favourite poems; perhaps write some ourselves; include some by Wilmot – and throw in a champagne reception."

"You couldn't make that a whisky tasting, I suppose," grunted the colonel. "Poetry's not my thing. I only know rugby songs and for that matter, so does the mayor. Rob and I used to play on the same team."

"I wandered lonely as a cloud," whispered Jilly.

"Half a league, half a league/Half a league onward," declaimed Cora.

"All in the valley of Death/Rode the six hundred," the colonel, replied. "Charge of the Light Brigade. Tennyson."

"That floats on high o'er vales and hills."

"See, Colonel, you do know poetry," continued Cora. "And it doesn't have to be daffodils. You could recite, 'The Charge.' Poets can be brave military people too. Rochester distinguished himself in the Dutch Wars after a cannonball blew his friends to pieces, right by his side."

"When all at once I saw a crowd/A host, of golden daffodils."

"Thank you, Jilly. We'll ask all the residents to choose their favourite poems and then we can perform them."

"But we'll still get a load of bloody daffodils," insisted the colonel.

"I shall read something by John Wilmot," said Cora. "He penned some beautiful love songs, but never about daffodils. He wrote all sorts of poems and understood they are for everyone and for all occasions."

"Beside the lake, beneath the trees/Fluttering and dancing in the breeze."

An hour later an exhausted Cora was recovering in her room, when Magda appeared. "I'll tidy up while you're having lunch. How was your first meeting?"

"Why do I do these things, Magda? We're planning a poetry anthology, that'll need some illustrations, including a picture of Rochester. Then on the day, we'll sell the anthologies and perform some of the poems. I'll also be needing musicians."

"What sort of music? My daughter, Natalie might be able to help. She's studying music and she'll be back from uni by April. She's a violinist and a lot of her friends are string players too, although her boyfriend plays classical guitar. He has the most incredibly long nails on one hand. It's really weird."

"He could have a purple beard and hobbit toes for all I care, so long as he can play some seventeenth century music – possibly at the champagne reception? Then the strings could play between the poems. Would that be possible?"

"I don't see why not. I'll call Natalie tonight, give her the date and we'll look at what we can do. Oh, and my brother-in-law's a printer, if you need one."

"What would I do without you, Magda? You're wasted in this place."

"The feeling's mutual, Cora. I'll see you tomorrow."

Cora sighed and put on a CD. There was a lot to be said for being so busy again, if only she could stay awake afterwards.

The cushions stirred.

"I recall this, Corinna. Another melancholy air."

"It's Dowland."

"You have had a great deal of talk concerning your masque?"

"I have indeed. It's called *Rochester Revived,* now. The poetry part is coming along fine, but I still have to organise the music – with Magda's help."

"Musicians are troublesome creatures. One endeavoured to replace all the court musicians with Englishmen, maintaining they quarrelled less than Frenchies, or Italiani. The king was enraged at the very thought. I encountered many

fine musicians in Italy, but I enjoyed the playing of their wives the more."

"I don't want to hear about that now, Johnny."

"I am glad I wrote of my encounters, so I can relive them."

"I'm beginning to think it's Memory Corner that's named after you, not Rochester House. Now let me show you which of your poems I'm thinking of including in the anthology. Have you finished the new one yet? I need to get it written down."

"Honour the charge they made/Honour the Light Brigade/Noble six hundred!"

The colonel looked absolutely magnificent in his full dress uniform and thunderous applause had greeted the final flourish of his, now frequently filled, champagne glass. He collapsed into his chair next to the mayor, as Jilly Townsend wafted to the microphone in pale yellow chiffon, clutching a bunch of daffodils.

This is going well, thought Cora.

There was such a good crowd, they had had to send out for more champagne and now everyone was in a relaxed mood. After Jilly's recitation and the string ensemble, the finale was Cora's performance and she was looking forward to it. Johnny would live again.

The Oxford Daily Echo – 3 April 2018

Visitors Stunned by Four-Letter Tirade at Home Recital
by our Staff Reporter, Sally Undercliffe

Visitors expecting an uplifting afternoon of poetry and music were stunned when an elderly lady unleashed a tirade of four-letter obscenities at them, after making claims she was descended from the poet who wrote them. Rochester House's manager apologised profusely for the upset, but said the lady was undergoing treatment at present. He had thought that organising the recital for the opening of the home's new wing would improve her condition, but it appears to have had the opposite effect.

The North Oxfordshire Gazette – 4 April 2018

Rochester Revived
by Our Community reporter, Matt Edwards

I have covered many events in retirement homes, but none quite like Rochester Revived, at Rochester House, last Saturday.

The afternoon began conventionally with a reception, ribbon-cutting and a welcome speech. Then in the new lounge, we were entertained to a poetry and music recital by the residents, and students from Warwick University. An illustrated anthology, with poems chosen and written by the residents and including poems by Restoration poet, John Wilmot, Earl of Rochester, after whom the house is named, was available to buy.

The recital began with a delicate performance for soprano and violin, from Sophie Dennett and Natalie Thompson, of

Burns' My love is like a red, red, rose. This was undoubtedly one of the afternoon's highlights, as was a particularly stirring performance of Tennyson, by a fully uniformed, Colonel Richard Drummond.

The final performer was Corinna Fordham, the organiser of the recital and she began with a beautiful poem by John Wilmot.

> 'Absent from thee I languish still
> Then ask me not when I return?
> The straying Fool will plainly kill
> To wish all Day, all Night to Mourn...'

Corinna explained she was named after a Greek poetess, when her father having spent several years, long before the computer age researching his family's history, discovered he was descended from John Wilmot.

"She never told us that," muttered the colonel, to the mayor.

Corinna praised her ancestor, who in spite of being portrayed as a rake and libertine who 'blazed out his health and youth in lavish voluptuousness,' was, to her, a misunderstood and much maligned figure, who deserved a higher place in the ranks of English literature.

In the next poem, she had the audience nodding along with the refrain, Ancient person of my heart, but pointed out that sometimes Wilmot went a little too far and she quoted from another of his works.

This was a different kind of love poem and finding four-letter words tumbling from the mouth of a beautifully dressed and rather forbidding lady, seemed surreal. As Corinna finished, there was silence. Possibly, if the string ensemble had struck up sooner – the players were actually stifling their laughter – all would have been well.

As it was, the colonel who had been flipping through the anthology, suddenly waved it in the mayor's face shouting "Dickhead! Look, I've just realised, it's not a face, it's lots of little interlaced dicks in a face shape. How clever's that?"

"It's a joke, Colonel," Corinna explained. "It's a treasure of the Ashmolean Museum. An Italian joke created on a plate. Usually, they were pictures of ladies' heads. I thought it complemented the Wilmot poem beside it, rather well."

"Complemented the poem?" spluttered the colonel, slapping the mayor on the back. Both of them bellowed with laughter. Some of the visitors, especially the younger ones, joined in, but others got up and headed for the door. Most of the residents were laughing, although a few just looked bewildered.

"We haven't finished," shouted Corinna. "I haven't read the poem my ancestor has especially written for us today."

The manager, looking highly embarrassed, searched for someone to apologise to, but seeing the mayor with tears running down his cheeks, hurried out after the disappearing visitors. By now, the strings were playing Purcell's 'When I am laid in earth,' a state Mr Plumrose probably hoped for at that point.

In the middle of this mayhem, I whisked Corinna off for an interview, which I reproduce in full below.

"You say your ancestor has written a poem for today?"

"Yes, Rochester Revived. He's written about returning home here, from Italy."

"Forgive me, but how's that possible when he's... been dead for almost four hundred and a half centuries?"

"He visits me. This is his house and I'm his ancestor. He's an apparition."

"A ghost."

"No, an apparition. He 'appears' to me because I'm his descendant and I know what he looks like from his portrait," she said pointing at the anthology's cover, "and of course, we're in his house.

This sounds very snobby, but most people would not recognise their sixteen times great ancestor even if they saw them, because they would not know what they looked like. I do, courtesy of the court portrait painter. I've never spoken about this before, but now I think that was the wrong decision. Johnny deserves to be appreciated."

"When did Rochester first appear to you?"

"The night I arrived here. I was feeling very sorry for myself, popped some early Purcell on the CD player and this person appeared, from under all the stuff heaped on my bed."

"So what was he wearing?"

"A nightshirt."

"A wig?"

"No, no, no. And the good news is – and something I've always wondered – is that you reveal yourself at the age you died, but whole. So if you died horribly mutilated, you won't scare anyone.

I asked him to write a poem for today. He recited it to me and I wrote it down, but now only the people who bought the anthology will see it. Please read it, print it and let me know what your readers think of it."

So, is Rochester House haunted by the ghost of the Earl of Rochester? Is Corinna Fordham suffering from some kind of hallucination? Or, was this just an April Fools' Day prank? Like I said, it was an event like none other. If you were there, let me know what you think. You can read the 'new' poem on page 15 and for those of a nervous disposition, there's only one four-letter word in it.

Is Rochester Really Revived?
by Our Community Reporter, Matt Edwards

A big thank you to those of you who attended Rochester Revived and have contacted me. There has been an interesting development in the last week. I sent the 'new' Rochester poem to a friend of mine at the university, who sent it to another friend who specialises in seventeenth century poetry and he says that the poem certainly could have been written by John Wilmot. So where does that leave us?

"This is part one of today's mail," said Magda, depositing armfuls of envelopes on Cora's bookcase. "The postman is still unloading the rest of it. Evidently there's even more comment on social media."

"I can't be bothered with that," said Cora. "I've more than enough letters, emails and phone calls to deal with. I've not finished yesterday's, yet. I've a letter from the mayor saying Saturday was the most enjoyable event he's attended all year and can he take me to lunch; *Haunted Oxfordshire* wants me to speak at their Annual Conference next month; I'm appearing on *South Today* tomorrow; the University Book Shop has been deluged with enquiries for Rochester's poetry; plus, I've two letters from the Ashmolean – one berating me for not asking their permission to reproduce what is now called 'Dickhead' – and another, thanking me for the long queues outside the museum to see the artefact. Oh, and three marriage proposals."

"Here's one letter you probably will want to open. It looks like it's from your son."

"It must be important, he usually emails me, but all in good time. Is Plumcake back from his 'holiday' yet?"

"The rumour is he may not return. He has a stress-related illness."

"I'm not surprised. The sheer cheek of the man lying to the press that I had a condition and then criticising me for bringing his home into 'disrepute,' (love the word) when he'd picked Robbie Burns as his favourite poet. Burns made Wilmot look like Pollyanna, but as he was a 'man of the people,' he was 'colourful,' not dissolute. Hypocrite! Plumcake wanted a memorable event and I gave him one."

"You're right, Cora, and evidently, there's been a rise in applications for places here."

Cora scanned her letter. "It seems my son has extended his Boston contract, will not be returning home this year, but hopes to come over for a flying visit in the summer."

"I'm sorry, Cora."

"Sorry! You have to be joking. I've had a whale of time recently. I'm staying here and having as many interviews, lunches and jollies that I can. I'm a batty old woman and I can do anything l want. I'm just off to the lounge for a meeting with the committee to plan our next event and then perhaps you could get me ready for my lunch date. I've been playing the recording Natalie's boyfriend made for us, so have a listen while you're clearing up. Your daughter's friends did brilliantly. They must come and play again. See you later."

Magda picked up a couple of stray letters from the carpet, turned up the CD player and began her ever more pointless tidying of Cora's bed.

"Again that dirge, Corinna!"

Magda dropped the bolster she was holding and stepped back.

"I'm not Cora."

Johnny's head appeared from underneath the cushions.

"I surmise you must be her Magda Maria. Another memory of my beloved Italy, it seems. I wish you good day, dear lady. Rochester is indeed revived."

About the author

Margaret Bulleyment began writing fiction and plays after a long career in comparative education. She has had short stories published in anthologies, including Chapeltown's *Café Lit*; *Snowflakes*; *Baubles* and *Glit-er-ary,* and on story websites.

As a finalist in the *Ovation Theatre Awards*, she has twice had short plays performed professionally. Her children's play *Caribbean Calypso* was runner-up in Trinity College of Music and Drama's 2011 International Playwriting Competition, and is available on TreePress. In December 2017, the play was performed three times in Bangalore, India, by *Jagriti Kids* – a charity promoting literacy and school attendance – for the children of migratory workers.

Crackers the Clown

Anne Wilson

I tried so hard to wish away his evil presence in my nightmares. If only that had worked. Once you're grown up, you stop trying.

Coulrophobia is 'an intense and irrational fear of clowns'. My fear is intense, but it has never been irrational, either then or now. I can still see the menace in Crackers black glossy eyes as he issued his invitation.

I can hear the droning buzz of summer insects, feel the dry summer heat, the warm, dry sand. And I remember something else, hot and sour-smelling, when my bare legs had tickled with a horrible accident.

I grew up in Fleetwood, in a house opposite the Marine Gardens with their Floral Hall and bandstand. There was a boating lake and large outdoor baths.

In the summer holidays, my younger brother and I spent most of our time on the beach with our buckets and spades building endless sandcastles; fascinated by seashells, worm-casts and little scuttling crabs, exploring around the rotting wooden drift-waters where strands of bladderwrack smelled of damp, like dead things.

On the hottest days our parents took us to the baths. Through the metal jaws of the turnstile, through un-lit changing rooms where your lungs stung with chlorine, and barefoot through a shallow trough of murky water which was supposed to prevent verrucas. It didn't; I got one anyway.

The most exciting thing we did was going to watch the marionette show.

There was a colonnaded area behind the baths, whitewashed, chalky and flaking, where people sat in their damp bathing suits on concrete blocks topped with green painted wooden slats. Jammed between the slats were beach pebbles, boiled sweet wrappers, cigarette filter tips, ice-lolly sticks and chewing gum.

Near these seats was the little marionette theatre; a wooden hut, painted green. Tightly shuttered up in winter, it was open all summer. On either side, a short flight of steps led to heavily curtained access at the rear of the stage. The theatre was backed by a curve of overgrown, very prickly Parks and Gardens rose bushes. In front, when the curtains were closed, a sign on a tripod stand had the time of the next performance slotted into it.

Arriving for the start of a performance, my brother and I would be given coins for the collection bag before hobbling barefoot over flinty ground in our clammy swimming costumes to claim one of the little folding seats.

We sat, teeth chattering, gritty sand between our toes; unaware of where our parents had gone, 'to have a cigarette', but confident they would always materialise to collect us when the show ended.

No-one ever ventured near the stage as it was impossible to know whether 'the man' was watching from somewhere. The man had waxy skin and sparse lank hair. He shuffled about wearing a long, stretched-looking cardigan. He took a collection in a grubby cloth bag halfway through the show and locked everything securely away afterwards. I don't remember ever hearing him speak, I think he just grunted.

All the marionettes were alarming. They were about the same size as us and sitting in front of the stage placed us roughly eye-level with their knees, looking up at them. As they swung and swished into view, their joints rattled, and they clattered their wooden feet across the boards like a troupe of clog wearers. Their painted facial expressions

47

were dramatic; their hair synthetic and untidy-looking, their costumes gaudy and fantastic.

They made an entrance, stage right, as their part of the fairy-tale was narrated by a disembodied voice, then made a dramatic exit, stage left, to the sounds of cheering or brave booing from their excited audience. Occasionally booing changed to screams as some characters would, without warning, raise their knees and together with much jangling and clashing, swing wildly outwards towards their critics, their supporting strings or wires disappearing into obscurity above.

The stage scenery consisted of a number of painted backdrops, faded and fraying with age, which dropped alarmingly from above like a rug being swiftly unrolled. They were interchangeable depending on the story; a large kitchen with a fireplace and a Welsh dresser, tree trunks in a wood, a fairy-tale palace, a cave. The marionettes were also interchangeable, each playing various roles.

There was one marionette which played a character in every story, Crackers the clown. This meant I held my breath through each performance, waiting for the cold shiver of fear he never failed to bring with him.

Crackers had a white head with a ruff of red frizzy hair. His black eyes had lines like wrinkles painted around them and his red mouth was very big. Sometimes I thought I could see teeth inside but other times I couldn't, so I supposed I had imagined them.

He often wore hats and cloaks to help give the impression of the character he was supposed to be, but you always knew it was him.

I learned that when Aladdin rubbed his lamp it was Crackers who appeared, not a genie. Little Red Riding Hood was confronted by Crackers, not a wolf, in her grandmother's bed. It was Crackers, not a witch, living in the gingerbread house in the woods, and Crackers who lived at the top of Jack's beanstalk, rather than the ogre I had read about.

Crackers was all-powerful which caused some of the stories to have bizarre twists but each one was related by the invisible storyteller in the same words time after time, like a record being played.

Always eager to impress my young brother, I had worked out that while the man was returning up the wooden steps with the collection bag, mid-performance, there was time to leave my seat and sneak up the steps on the opposite side. As these steps were hidden from view by the rose bushes, I should be able to creep up and peek inside at floor level during the second half of the performance. I knew, if caught I would be in trouble but once having imagined myself doing it I had to see it through. I instructed my brother to remain firmly on his seat throughout my adventure or risk my refusing to play with him ever again.

As usual, halfway through the performance the bag of coins was jiggled in front of us. My brother and I added our offering and the man shuffled past. I made my move.

The rose bushes were densely packed and had fine sharp thorns. However, they were quite large and mature, leaving just enough space at ground level for a crouching child to scramble through. My ill-fitting, outgrown swimming costume offered little protection, but I thought of the scratches I received as badges of courage to show off to my brother. Insects tickled my perspiring skin and sandy dirt stuck to it.

I located the wooden steps and started up them, taking great care to keep my head down. The audience settled as the performance resumed. I squatted, my head level with the top step, gathering my courage whilst deciding how best to proceed. This close to the stage, the noise was much louder; the marionette's feet on the boards sounded thunderous. It was the first time I remember ever being aware of my heart beating inside my rib-cage.

Directly in front of me was heavily draped curtaining. By lifting it a fraction I saw I was roughly in line with the stage's painted backdrop in front of which the marionettes swung and cavorted. Behind this, in a darkened area, I imagined there to be all sorts of secrets. It was towards this private space that I first edged my head under the curtain's hem.

Stale air parched my throat. The cramped space contained metal frames like clothes rails on which a few familiar characters hung waiting in the gloom. They looked as if at any moment they might slowly raise their heads or stretch a hanging arm out towards me.

Half-closed cardboard boxes were piled haphazardly about and, in an old armchair, was slumped the figure of the man. He appeared to be sleeping while a recording related the story of Little Red Riding Hood to the audience outside. On a table sat a half full glass of something and what looked like a curling sandwich. I took in all these details, memorising particulars, with which to impress or scare my brother, before it occurred to me that something was wrong.

Close by, a little platform ran behind the scenery backdrops from which to stand and dangle the marionettes. It was deserted. I could see no-one but the sleeping man. Curious as to how the animation was achieved, I carefully withdrew my head and chose a different section of curtain hem from under which to peep. My eye-line followed the dusty boards of the stage where the scene was set for Little Red Riding Hood to enter Grandma's house. My nemesis, Crackers, was in position beneath a sheet on Grandma's bed.

As I stared transfixed, Crackers turned his head slowly and deliberately in an action impossible for a marionette. The glare from the pitch-black eyes froze me where I crouched. They held a flicker, like a lick of amber flame, igniting a terrible fear in me; a fear I would never, in my whole life, be able to articulate. Far worse than fear of discovery by the man, far worse than the wrath of my father, far worse than anything I was capable of imagining.

I wished myself at home with my parents, at school with teachers, anywhere but on these wooden steps surrounded by the spiny thorns of rose bushes, exposed and damned, looking at something I should never have seen.

Crackers somehow managed a grotesque smile; how was this possible? The smile communicated soundlessly; words inside my brain, 'you have discovered us... do come again. We will all be waiting for you.'

I don't remember scrambling down and back to my brother. I remember him protesting and crying as I dragged him away. I remember my parents' concern and the endless questions.

"Did the man say something?", "Did someone do something?", and "Did you use the outside toilet by yourself?"

My answers were always negative, and the questions stopped eventually. Of course, I was being asked the wrong questions, but it made no difference as I had no words to describe my absolute terror of ever watching the marionettes again after that day.

I remember the subsequent relief and enthusiasm with which I embraced our family's move to another town the following year; a midland town, a reassuringly safe distance away from seaside attractions and entertainments. I thought secretly that perhaps the move would end the nightmares, but I was to be disappointed. Since then, I have woken countless times with night-sweats, half delirious with fear.

Now I have joined my grandchildren's seaside holiday. We are far away from the home of my childhood, but the wooden theatre, the shabby hut with weathered green paintwork is here. It stands in a sheltered corner of the lower promenade, looking as if it has always been here, looking exactly the same. It sits adjacent to a kiosk selling whipped ice cream, cold fizzy drinks and inflated foil dolphins. Arranged in rows in front are, if I remember correctly, the same small chairs.

Most seats are already filled as little Tom and his big brother, Charlie, eagerly drag me to the back row. From somewhere hidden, music begins to play; fairground, hurdy-gurdy music. Beneath my gingerly distributed weight, the feet of the little chair grate alarmingly on a gritty ground-cover of windblown sand.

I place a protective arm behind my grandchildren. Rattling windmills, whirling outside the kiosk, seem to have entered my head. My heart hurts inside my chest. My skin dampens as the curtains open. Charlie and Tom gasp with excitement as Aladdin's cave is revealed.

The story begins. At the front of the stage Aladdin rubs a magic lamp. My back stiffens, and my mouth is dry. My grip tightens on the back of Tom's seat. Much unseen clashing and jangling, heralds the approach of the genie.

A swish of shiny black brocade and a large figure swings on to the stage. On his head he wears a jewelled turban. He has kohl-black eyes, and long curling fingernails. He is not as big as me; he does not look at me.

I exhale slowly, shrinking into my seat. My arms go limp.

I now see that these marionettes are new, not shabby as I remembered them. They have glossy faces and bright polyester clothes. Then I see the theatre is not in fact how I remembered it at all; the seats similar but not the same.

My grandchildren belong to a different age. For them, the fairy tales are still the same, but the marionettes are only big dolls with strings, not darkly dingy and menacing as I remembered them, not the stuff of nightmares.

When the show is over, a foreign-looking man emerges carrying the genie. He offers a photo-opportunity to his young audience. I get out my camera-phone and Tom and Charlie pose eagerly.

Afterwards, as we push our way through the small crowd, the puppet's dangling hand grazes mine sharply and I wonder if splintered wood or perhaps one of its long fingernails might have been responsible when I see it has drawn blood.

Back at home, Charlie and Tom view the photograph I took, giggling at the sight of themselves beside a genie they find comical.

I look over their shoulders. To my horror, I see my grandchildren's laughing faces next to a white face with wisps of frizzy red hair escaping from under its jewelled turban. Sharp-looking teeth are definitely visible inside the red, grinning mouth. The image shivers slightly and the grin grows wider.

Crackers is still in charge of his troop.

My skin feels clammy and the recent scratch on my hand itches where a dirty looking scab has formed. I am a boy again. I am wishing as hard as I can.

About the author
Anne grew up on the west coast of England and in the north east where she taught literacy and art in junior schools. She also lived for several years in Mallorca. These locations have inspired her writing, most of which involves an otherworldly element entering the lives of ordinary people. She achieved a BA Hons in Advanced Creative Writing in 2010, since when her fiction has appeared regularly in anthologies. These include Bridge House's *Light in the Dark* and a proposed single author collection of dark stories to be published by Bridge House. She also has two completed novels looking for a home.

Cracks in the Mirror

Sally Angell

Open the door. Make an entrance. *You're good at that!*

I've rehearsed this moment so many times, whenever passing a reflective surface, trying to get back into role. It's like putting on an old dress, or rather skirt and blouse. There she is, that girl you used to know. But getting into her head again is another matter.

She's still shadowy, Maddy, in the background behind the stronger image of Adele who is me, myself, today. How to get Now Me to morph into Then Me? It's doing my head in. I've been hyperventilating at night. 'No no *no.'*

Is it worth it? When the e-invitation arrived, my fingers hovered over Delete. It was a long way to travel in winter. And you heard horror stories about these old girls' reunions. But I knew I would go. It's some masochistic need. I've read about this Exposure Therapy. Bite the bullet, face the fear full on. Exorcise those demons for good.

So I RSVP'd back, accepting. And a few panic attacks ago bumped the Audi through the gateway of St. Helena's, into the playing fields. I mean car park. With the reduced outdoor lighting, I felt I'd stepped into one of those dark Noir dramas, where present and flashback scenes are confused.

"Hi." Other figures were emerging from cars, in a swish of skirts, jeaned legs, the flash of an earring. For these occasions, it was dress to impress 'see how successful/happy/normal I have turned out.'

I waved, but rounded the corner alone to the school façade, its familiar architecture stark against black sky. Gothic turrets towered like a portent in one of the nineteenth-century novels we had to pretend to understand on long sleepy, hormonal English Lit afternoons. I was re-entering the haunting landscape of a thousand fevered dreams.

I repeated the researched blurb to myself like a mantra. "St. Helena's is no longer a secondary school. In the nineteen-nineties it became an adult education establishment,' blah blah, 'and now caters for conferences, training days, and private study breaks. Rooms are available for hire.'"

I reminded myself. *It's only a building. You can always run. No one can make you stay. No one can make you do anything.* And it was true. Is true. The rules have changed. There are no rules; except in the subconscious landscape of our collective memory. Those who were there.

As my boot heels clicked into the entrance hall the *same* even duller green-grey tiles I was caught between two worlds. One was the black and white movie of, 'And did those fee – ee – t…' sung with the strange pent up passion of adolescent girls on the cusp. The other was the insulated domain of a wife, mother, and online trader.

In Reception, a marker-pen arrow pointed the way. Energy-saving bulbs cast only a pall in the darkness. Everything seemed smaller. I dream-walked towards the area booked for tonight's event. And that was when I began to psyche myself into character… *Open the door. Make your entrance…*

Oops! In a bump of boobs and cloud of Avon, I'm thrust into sudden intimacy with someone in the shadows. A badge gleams up. *The Greeter.* Do I know her? Is she one of us, or one of the venue staff? The lived-in features and figure could belong to any fifty-something woman. And I realize that in addition to matching each face to the right person after so long, we'll need to do a quick mental age-reversal in order to recognize anyone.

"Welcome."

Nah, the voice doesn't chime any bells either. She hooks my coat onto a peg, offers a tray of identity stickers. Christian names only, I notice, rummaging through the Linda's, Karen's, Mary's and all the other popular monikers of that year. But it makes sense, because surnames will mostly have changed.

"Where's mine?" Another scrabble through the stickers. Airbrushed out! But then, why invite me? I fight down paranoia, as sticker and pen are slapped into my hand. Resting the plain strip in my other palm I scribble on it, and slap the gluey side to the sparkly sweater I got off eBay. Right. Got to do this. Ready!

This really is it, then. I'm stepping over the carpet rod into what was the canteen, if I've remembered the internal geography. Big diaphragm breath. Grasp the knob. Turn it. Push!

Ta-dah!

A big silence. In the dull orange glow, a cluster of women stand awkwardly, making conversation. Are they wondering which Lisa or Laura or Donna this is? Best friends, arch enemies. It's a minefield. We must all be masochists.

I brace myself, inner organs buckling as memories unleash. Should have gone for the elastic-waisted skirt after all, and popped a handful of Kalms. I spy liquid refreshment in the corner where the tuck-shop used to be, and head for that instead.

"Punch!" An egg-shaped woman with fuchsia ringlets is gaily swishing orangey liquid and fruit round in a bowl. "Avec alcohol, but we also have ze soft drinks, coffees, teas, herbal and otherwise."

Adele rarely drinks. She's heeded all the warnings. But Maddy craves anything to null twanging nerves. I swig down a mouthful, and grin at the barwoman.

"Don't tell me. Hang on Julie Mayhew?"

The crooked teeth have been straightened out but are still like irregular tombstones. She chuckles, points at her sticker.

"I would know you anywhere," I chirp, feeling better with every mouthful as the cocktail of prosecco, wine, spirits, whatever, starts to spread its anaesthetic. It's all right. Everything's good. And even if it isn't, I'm quite safe. I can step out of this historical fiction, and go home.

A crowd bursts through the door, in that explosion of oestrogen typical of all-female gatherings. Were there really this many of us in Class of 19 - -?

A trestle table (it *can't* be that one from the gym?) lurches in the centre of the space where dinner tables used to be laid each day, four places a side, a prefect from sixth form at each end. I suddenly taste the oniony mince in my mouth, of spag bol on Tuesdays and Thursdays.

There's a box of cosmetics, and set of canvas and wools at one end of the trestle. Perhaps we'll be treated to a make-over. Or a cross-stitch demo. 'Bring something to share," the confirmation email had stated. What sort of something? Perhaps for a group game or activity, in case the intensity of too much recall brings on hot flushes. I slam my carrier bag down on the scratched wood.

"Crackers!"

A noise like a donkey on steroids makes me jump.

"Ha. Ha. How apt. You always were completely *Crackers!* Look who it is, girls – mad, bonkers, crackers, nutty as a fruit cake Maddy!"

Wham. Bang. She's back, that girl who learnt survival skills. I spin round.

"Well, hello, *Honker!* Nice to see you, too. I mean of course, *hear* you." Mouths fall open, half-laughing, half gapes of fear. The nickname was always whispered, but no one ever dared say it to foghorn voice herself. Not to the bully of 5B.

We stare each other out, me and the tormentor I used to hide in cupboards to avoid. Then with another ear-shattering bray, she turns away to target someone else. But I've been recognized, and am now bombarded with cries of "Maddy! Mads! Mad! How are you?"

I'm saved by a stranger with a big S stitched on her left lapel and an R or is it a P? on the right one.

"Hi everyone. I'm Melanie from Schoolfriends Reunited." Sniggers at the reference to the original site, where many of us will have traced bessie mates and, covertly, old flames. "A friend and I," Melanie smiles, "started our Reunion Planning company in two thousand and eleven. We're sort of like wedding planners, not for nuptials, but for events that bring schoolmates back together, to laugh and cry over the best days of your life, and all that."

I'm searching round for one face that hasn't appeared yet. The two of us were the outsiders of our year: me with my fooling around, and Jenni, like my shadow, quiet and compliant. The gap beside me, here, without her, is palpable.

"It's not always comfortable going back," Melanie finds her prompt card. "We always remember our own excruciating times of embarrassment, our own traumas and faux pas." Complimentary laughter. "But when we have shared (some may say suffered!) life experiences with a particular set of people, it's a unique relationship. So I'll let you get on now and have fun."

The food at one end of the table is uncovered, and we stand or sit round, with plastic plates, stuffing our faces with sandwiches and salads, sushi and quinoa bites, cookies, chocolate gateaux. "D'you remember that time when we…"

Attention turns to the entertainment. Items of all sorts are jumbled at that end of the table now, causing much curiosity, and hilarity at a box of "toys." Someone examines my offering.

"Oh, crackers."

"Yeh, I've got an online company, novelties.com." I feel carefree and giggly, from the bonhomie and the earlier booze. "Go on, pull one."

Bang!

"Who's this?" the holder of the joke end reads out. *"A Hose by any other name, would smell just as sweet."* A tinkle of laughter. "Dear Maddy. Still fooling around."

I rubber my face into clown mode. "Just testing."

Perhaps I've gone too far with the reference to the ex-pupil with a personal freshness issue, but thankfully she isn't here.

Another bang, and a sharp whiff of sulphur.

"Busty. Who has EE cups?"

A few nervous titters. Eyes swivel to the montage on the wall. *Absent Friends.* I see the picture. Laura Exley. The pink ribbon over the corner. OMG. Is she dead?

"Sorry! I'm *so* sorry." I snatch up the torn red crepe paper and contents.

"Laura's doing well." A quiet voice. "She's finished the chemo. Always smiling, and so positive."

Mortified, I stuff the rest of the tailor-made crackers away. Perhaps Julie's makeovers will be more successful. And over in the corner, a few people with their own knees are wobbling on one leg on yoga mats, and making moaning noises.

I almost forget why I'm here. But somewhere outside these walls in the cold and the dark, the secret waits, and the question that needs to be answered. Perhaps I can make my excuses, and go.

A touch on my shoulder makes me freeze.

"You're Maddy Moore, aren't you? I've spoken to everyone else.' Anxious eyes fasten on mine. "My hair's grown back."

"That's good. That's *good,"* I smile. *Who the hell is she?*

"It was alopecia. I had to wear a wig." I look more closely. Yes. I remember her now, and her thick brown mane. But I never knew.

"Love the barnet now."

"Thanks." Her eyes light up with pride as she strokes the grey bob.

The table's overflowing with mangled serviettes, half-eaten sausage rolls, and tipped over wine glasses. Born-again teenagers have relaxed into themselves again, after the diarrhoea-stirring encounters with people who remembered them as someone else.

There's a sense of rightness, as if we've come full circle, as if our paths have followed a natural pattern. And we realize that our lives, unexpectedly, make sense. I like it. We have each lived and are still living, a proper story. And a chapter of that was our time at St Helena's together.

The punch must be wearing off. I only had one glass. Adele doesn't drink-drive. But it leaves me a bit flat. Mustn't forget why I'm *really* here. My head's fuzzy now. It's puzzling. Nobody's said anything. And someone *must* know what happened. It was in the papers.

I'd just like to go home, before the mellowness wears off. But I can't back out now. Just got to get it over with. I make a quick exit, grab my coat, and a torch from my purse and slip outside, turning left by the science block as was.

I step onto the path, feet vibrating with all those

footprints buried beneath, going forwards, backwards, and retracing endlessly. I find myself passing the ghosts of pupils scattered about the grounds. And me in my blue cotton dress.

It was the day before the exams. As I sweated up to the pavilion, heat scorched my skin. The sickly scent of roses from the garden wall mixed with the burny smell of the ciggy in my hand; my first one. Already stressed to high heaven, I cried with the frustration of trying to inhale, not getting it right, and choking.

I pushed the door of the pavilion, and it gave. The test papers were laid out on the desks for morning. I backed out, gasping for air, somehow dropping the fag. I heard the click of the borrowed lighter as I put it down on the wall, and then nothing.

Snap! Like crackers when two people pull in opposite directions, to breaking point. Crack! Something went off inside my head. Couldn't do it anymore. All the trying to make the right shapes on the page. Even the question paper, with the printed letters dancing and changing places, was meaningless.

This was pre extra time, and without audio or digitally helpful options. There were no orange glasses, or support assistants to act as scribes. Just the question, an indecipherable jumble. And the page, a white blank for writing the answer...

Here in that spot that has haunted me for so long, I can't believe it. Modern windows have replaced the old panes, but the long, low single-storey building itself is here. Still standing. Just as it was! I've always skipped any news postings about St Helena's that might be distressing, even though I wanted to know.

The strains of the Conga reach my ears, and discordant singing of "la la lalala la la." Arms and legs of my old classmates are dancing in all directions down the steps of the school.

"Madeleine."

I blink, taking in the black hair, now snow-streaked, the pale face and skinny figure. Here she is, at last, the girl who covered for me, who understood why I flipped when teachers asked me to read.

"Jenni?"

"I couldn't face all that." She grimaces towards the school. The words tumble out. She doesn't live far away, she says. But she had to come. "Thought you might be here."

I stare. Pictures are forming, filling in the mental block that has never cleared. Regaining consciousness, I'd seen and heard flames. I was vaguely aware of someone else there. But I'd run, walking for two hours to get home. After months of strain, I collapsed and didn't go back.

"It was *you.*" I still don't get it.

"I wanted to be different, make something happen. I wasn't like you, able to joke about things. I saw the lighter, and I wanted to burn down the whole school."

"But the fire?" All the years of worry, my mind reeling: the cigarette. And was there someone inside, maybe, at a locker, or in the cloakroom?

"It wasn't really a fire." She'd put the flames out with the extinguisher. There was slight damage to some books just inside the pavilion, they had changed the exam to another room, and it was mentioned in the local paper, but that was it.

I try to take it in, as Jenni fills in the pieces of the puzzle. The police put it down to vandals. The school closed. We'd heard about the funding changing, and it did. So no one went back in September. She'd phoned my house but no one answered.

We're hurrying back now. Lights are going out.

Everyone's leaving, locking up the building. Jenny hangs back, says she'll slip out of the other exit. We've swapped numbers. But I don't know.

"Bye Maddy," voices call out on the night air. "See you again."

But they won't. I feel that girl letting me go, fading back into the bricks, echoing through the walls and corridors. And I let her go.

Goodbye Maddy.

About the author

Sally Angell loves literature and writing, and is always aiming to develop new and original ideas in her work. Sally explores the truth and reality of feelings, the originality of language and the possibilities of words. She likes to write stories with contemporary themes that also have a universal meaning. Her writing has been published in magazines and anthologies, and read on radio.

In Plain Sight

Kay Middlemiss

Tap... tap... tap... "Come on, come on," words whispered through half closed lips.

Tap... tap... tap... sensitive fingers on scarred, grey metal; touching, searching, listening for the pulse hidden beneath the surface.

Tommy Price, perched on the corner of a dusty office chair where he could watch without being a distraction, pulled the thin fabric of his demob jacket closer for what little warmth it gave, crossed and uncrossed his arms trying to ignore the knot in his gut. This was taking too long.

Suddenly Neddy sat back on his heels. The light from his head-torch drawing a beam across the dark space, over the betting slips and pre-war horse-racing photographs that covered the walls, rested on the anxious frown of his accomplice. "Can't be done."

"What d'you mean, 'can't be done'?" He was joking, surely. Neddy was the best cracker in the business. Everyone said so.

"I said, 'can't be done'. Don't you understand plain English? It might be old and scruffy but it's got some mechanism that's stopping me getting in. Anyway," Neddy went on, "I'm not so sure there is a fortune in there. Think about it. Would you leave a stash in an empty building that's due for demolition?"

Tommy thought about it. "Hide things in plain sight, that's what they say. Nobody'd be daft enough to try and crack a safe like that."

"We did."

"Ah, yes, well, I had information, didn't I?" Tommy sniffed the stale air: fag ash, pale fumes from a paraffin heater, old sweat… this room was not dead. Someone still used it. Someone would be back – back for the contents of the safe they couldn't open. To be so near, thanks to all his careful planning and be denied the prize, didn't sit well with Tommy Price, part time businessman and cat-burglar. "But there's a fortune in there."

Neddy shrugged. "Could be the crown jewels, I still can't get into it."

"There must be a way." Tommy jumped off the chair and walked round the safe, meticulously examining every inch. "There'll be a weak spot. Always is." He stopped at the back of the metal box. "A 'cetylene torch! Forget the lock, Neddy. We'll go in through the back door."

"An acetylene torch? If you knew where to lay your hands on one…"

"I do."

"No. This place may be due for demolition but that's not my line of business."

"You're right. It's too risky to do it here. We'll take her across to O'Riley's scrap yard." It would mean splitting the profit three ways but even a third of what was in that safe was better than nothing. "Here, give us a hand to walk it to the door."

"And then what? Do you think no one's going to notice if we walk it down the street, even at this time of night?"

"Know what you're saying. Wheels. We need a set of wheels. She's too heavy to carry." Tommy thumped his forehead with the heel of his hand. "In the garage! Of course, there's a van in the garage next door. I can get it running. The door will be a piece of cake for you. We'll be round at O'Riley's in five minutes."

The garage door opened easily but inside lay something Tommy had not anticipated. Instead of a van the floorspace was covered with packing cases, tea chests and a stack of wooden crates. "He's done a runner!"

The beam of Neddy's torch came to rest on a ring of white rubber. Metal spokes gleamed. "You wanted wheels," said Neddy. "If it's what I think it is there'll be a second pair just about… here."

"But it's a pram!"

"Yeah, it's a pram. What could be more innocent than Grandad pushing a baby's pram up the street?"

"You mean with a safe in it, all tucked up in a blanket, nice and cosy?"

"Penny finally dropped, has it? Come on, let's get these packing cases out of the way."

The crates were light and piled up haphazardly, almost reached the roof. Tommy began to manoeuvre the pram out into the cleared space but there was another box blocking his way – a large, metal box.

"Shine the torch down here," he commanded. "There's some writing on this one. What's it say?"

"Explosives. W.D.," Neddy read out. "I don't believe it!"

"War Department." Tommy smiled to himself. "He was well into the black market. Shame we can't make use of it but I was in Catering Corps not Demolition. Though some of the blokes did say it was the same thing. Give us a hand to lift it on top of the pile. Now for the serious business. We'll take the pram round to the back door and load up the safe. We pass O'Riley's place on the way to the yard. I'll give him a knock."

The street lights were back on but the town's residents, thanks to the blackout years, had got used to not looking out of their windows. No one noticed the two men furtively pushing a pram along the street that night.

Mrs O'Riley was to be the next problem. She absolutely refused to wake her husband who was having an early night

66

after a heavy day. Tommy cajoled and threatened but it was Neddy's intervention that solved the situation.

"Wouldn't you like to go back to the old country for a nice long holiday? Stay in a posh hotel, all expenses paid?"

Mr O'Riley was up and dressed before they'd had time to drink the tea his wife had made for them.

At the O'Riley premises the safe was offloaded from the pram and given a second careful examination. "No problem, lads." O'Riley, who would be the tool operator, could hardly believe his luck. A safe full of money had just walked right into his yard.

The explosion shook the earth. It flattened the shed that was the office and scattered parts and debris into the surrounding streets and allotments. The noise was deafening. It was a miracle, they said, that no one had been seriously injured. Tommy and Neddy were released from hospital later that day with bandaged hands. O'Riley probably fared the worst having to suffer the wrath of Mrs O'Riley. The fire brigade made a note in their log that the three men had done more damage to the neighbourhood in one night than Hitler had managed in six years.

"That's some reputation," Tommy grumbled, "for a cat-burglar."

There were sniggers at the police station too where the men were charged. "What self-respecting burglar would try to blow open a safe full of explosive?" the arresting officer asked Neddy. "A right bunch of crackers we've got here, Serge."

In a derelict garage, not a million miles away from O'Riley's yard, the explosion caused a pile of haphazardly stacked crates to shift their position. A large metal box that had lain on the top of the pile, came crashing to the floor. The impact shattered the lock and as the lid opened, a flimsy rectangle of white paper fluttered to the floor. It was followed by another slip of paper, then another, and another until there was a sizable pile of paper on the garage floor. Each piece was identical; each had printing and carried a watermark, and on each slip was an imprint of King George's head.

About the author
After a career in the airline industry Kay settled on the Isle of Anglesey. She is a founder member of Copper Writers creative writing group and has been involved with the Montage publications of two bi-lingual anthologies of Anglesey writers and poets. In September 2017 she helped launch the first Writing Festival on the island. Her haunted house and spaniel Megan have been the inspiration for many of her stories.

Dress Form

Christopher Bowles

And it's softer than I thought it would be.

Softer, yet somehow heavier.

There's a weight in the drop of the fabric; a sort of... purpose, in the way the material moved. Each swish of the skirt gave the impression of dignified movement. The poised leg of a prima donna, the tilted wrist of a geisha, the firm salute of the maestro. It was somehow full of movement and music and... emotion, even when it was still.

On the mannequin in the shop window, it looked somehow both innocent and dignified. Childlike and royal. Virginal yet epicene. And that was what drew my eye, I guess. The fact it managed to somehow represent a tightly woven bundle of contradictions, yet never looked... I'm not sure how to describe it really. I'm usually quite eloquent, but when it comes to this dress... somehow words fail me every time.

It was like the tailor had left a blank canvas. A black sheet of material that could be anything, and everything. And every time I saw it from the very first day, a small fire inside me was fed, and fanned, and burned.

I had passed it by a month ago. I was cramping all through my shift, and just wanted to curl up with a trashy bodice-ripper, a hot water bottle and a tub of cookie-dough ice-cream. It had been snowing for the last week, and predictably, the Underground was in complete disarray. I was forced into the streets with a crowd of other commuters, mumbling and grumbling and shouting nonsensically into mobile phones. Those dreaded three words.

Replacement Bus Service

And in that short walk from the underpass, the hot air from the station billowing out and around me, up cavernous stairs, and into the frigid street… I saw it. From across the road, in between blurs of passing traffic. And I couldn't place it exactly. That feeling. But I had forgotten about the inconvenience, and the gnawing ache below my stomach. I was no longer contemplating a strawberry cheesecake instead of ice-cream. Instead, I was alone in a street, watching a shop window. And something in the window was watching me.

My reverie was interrupted by the push of the throng behind me, and I struggled to fight against the flow of people. But my temporary lapse was soon forgotten, and I swam along with the crowd, moving with the current until it dispersed up against posters on temporary bus terminals. A thousand impatient eyes seeking the right service to get home.

When I finally had my key in the lock, something gnawed away at the back of my mind. Something other than the ice-cream I'd forgotten to buy, and tomorrow's deadline. But I simply couldn't place it.

The next week passed by unremarkably. Life went on. Alarm clocks were reset, coffees were chugged at keyboards, and Aunt Flo kept her visit blissfully short. Meetings were planned, postponed and cancelled. Trains were boarded, alighted, delayed. The snow continued to fall, and time continued to tick away. I came back to an empty house, but was not sad. I had a very comfortable life. I liked my job, and I liked that I wasn't single. I was just between relationships, post-divorce, and very happy on my own. I didn't own any cats, or dogs, or any animals, really. No kids, no hobbies to speak of. In my earlier years, I had dreamt of creating costumes for the theatre. I had taken sewing lessons, and bought many dress-forms, and still had an old pre-war Singer up in the attic. Probably gathering dust with a basket full of pincushions, spools of ribbon and thread. But in the end, like most hobbies... it fell to the wayside. And was swiftly forgotten, replaced by dentist appointments, and hair colourings, and the metronome rhythm of the nine-to-five.

I watched the inside of the tunnel speed by until my vision swam. The gentle rocking of the train lulling me into calm. When the doors opened, and the passengers spilled out onto the platform, we were once again greeted with whiteboards and a neat scrawl.

Replacement Bus Service

Swept along by a faceless sea back up into the crisp air, I caught snatches of conversations meant for private ears. And I found myself pre-emptively looking across the road as we emerged from the mouth of the Underground. I could feel the swell of people pushing me down the street, but my head refused to follow my feet. I kept staring back, but not quite sure at what.

The next day; the same routine.

> Alarm, coffee, eggs.
> Meetings, clipboards, reports.
> Clock in, clock out, coat and keys in hand.
> Lather, rinse, repeat.

But this time, I stood on the connecting platform with all the other suits and skirts. All the other grey nobodies.

All of the drones. And when the familiar whistle came down the tunnel – the distant roar of the train as it shunted and squealed its way to us… I froze.

The people parted around me, and jostled for seats in the carriage, prodding each other with umbrellas and briefcases. And I looked through the window as every passenger armed themselves for the journey. Legs were splayed too far apart to hoard space. Newspapers were unfolded and took up too much room. Compacts were opened, lipstick reapplied. MP3-players and paperbacks and smartphones.

The doors remain opened for a tantalising few seconds. I could feel myself longing to step forward, and join the hubbub. Slip back into my place amongst the monotonous many. But I didn't. The doors slid shut, and an eyebrow or two was raised at my awkward stance. Not many. But enough to feel self-conscious. It pulled away, the backdraught blowing my hair about my face.

I expect I was forgotten by the time it reached the next station; witnesses reintegrating themselves into the private familiarity of chapters and text messages and the latest chart-topping love songs.

I stood there for a minute or two, before my feet seemed to move of their own accord. One in front of the other, tiled walls creating optical illusions in front of my swimming eyes. Then the ticket barrier, stairs, and a stretch of pavement covered in old chewing gum and cigarette butts.

I felt myself looking up, in a direction I already knew, at a shop window I had already seen.

And I crossed the road.

I pressed myself up against the glass, like a child drooling over sherbet saucers and aniseed. I don't recall what the shop was called, or what it sold, or even how much

I paid. But this time, when my key slipped into the lock, I was holding a plain black bag, containing a black dress that was anything but ordinary.

"What a cracker."

The words slipped out of his mouth like cigar smoke. His bottom lip twisted like a hungry leech, and I thought he might be trying to smile.

My father never smiled. He was a very serious man, and spoke with remarkable thrift – no word was ever wasted. Not on things like compliments, or gratitude, or pleasantries. He never even responded to 'hello' with anything more than a pre-occupied grunt; and as a girl, I always used to wonder what my mother saw in him.

"You look like a china doll. A cracking, china doll..."

Again, the words seemed to slip from him in surprise. As if they slid from his control, unleashed by a rebellious tongue. His own confusion seemed to melt away when he saw my own; spread unabashedly across my features. He patted his knee reassuringly, urging me closer.

I clambered onto his lap, arranging my dress around me, and giving it my full attention. I had never sat on his knee before, and it should have been a wonderful occasion. But I could smell the smoke and the whiskey on his breath from the doorway, and it made me uneasy.

Even at six years old, I knew a bad thing was about to happen. Something that would make me squirm, inside and out. But I didn't know any better. Couldn't have found the words to describe how I felt before, during or after it happened.

He caught my hand as I smoothed out the folds of my skirts on his thigh. And he held it there, refusing to let go.

I awoke with a start.

Disoriented, I tried to place my surroundings, and

realised I had fallen asleep in the lounge, on a battered armchair that still smelt vaguely like my mother's perfume. I smiled wanly to myself, and as I sat up, I realised the dress was draped over me like a quilt. I let my fingers roam over the fabric, stroking the grain of the material both ways, enjoying the different textures I found there.

I nestled further into the back of the chair, staring into space, and caressing the material.

Can a dress feel sad?

The question was ridiculous, I know. But it popped into my head involuntarily. I couldn't explain it, but the material, so heavy and almost (but not quite) velvet, just seemed to radiate something almost mournful. When I stroked it, I felt my eyelids and arms growing heavy, as if I just wanted to curl up in a ball and die. But somehow, it felt... familiar. Almost a... happiness? A happy kind of sad? Underneath the dress, I should have been hot, but I wasn't uncomfortable. But my left leg was going numb, and so I readjusted myself, stretching out and furling back up furtively.

A happy sadness. That's the closest thing to describing what this is.

It was a definite dignity. Every shift of the material felt purposeful, confident. So much so, I could feel my own timidness in comparison. I was enraptured by the dress, but almost terrified to put it on. So instead, I held it, and tried to remember what I'd been dreaming about.

Checking the clock, I saw how early it was. My alarm for work wouldn't be buzzing insistently for at least another hour and a half.

So instead, I just lay there.

In the chair.

The arms of the little black dress wrapped tightly around me.

On the train to work, I began to think of my father. I stared at the shoes of strangers on the opposite seat, and struggled to remember what sort of clothes he used to wear. Was he all suits and brogues? Or was he a work-boots and overalls man? The details seemed to dance away from me, every time they seemed within reach. But I could remember small things. The way he'd wrinkle his nose after he drank his morning orange juice, shaking small droplets from his moustache. The way he'd tap out his pipe on the coffee table, and my mother would fuss and tut, but never scold him. His favourite colour was blue. Until he turned sixty-four, and had a severe stroke. His memory came back in bits and pieces, and he'd tell the nurses on a daily basis that his favourite colour was red. Until it was green. Then purple. Then brown.

But he was stubborn. A fighter. And even though his mind was addled and failing, his body was strong and healthy, and I wondered when he might finally give up. He was nearly eighty now – a fine age for anyone in today's world, let alone someone as fragile as him. Nowadays, he only wore pyjamas and dressing gowns and slippers, and simply tottered around from room to room in the home, talking to houseplants, and wall-clocks and the nurses when they took his blood pressure. And every day, it was the same routine.

Talk to the ficus. 140/90. My favourite colour is yellow.

Talk to the yucca. 138/87. My favourite colour is turquoise.

75

Talk to the wall-clock. 139/90. My favourite colour is black…

You could wear your new dress to the funeral.

I smile in spite of myself, I didn't hate my father. Not even for the things he had done. It was difficult to explain, even to myself – but just as I was a six-year-old girl who didn't know better, so was he. He just had a few decades-worth of experience. But he was lost. Naive and wandering, maybe; waiting for someone to show him right from wrong.

At the office; the same routine.

> Briefings, charts and figures.
> Meetings, clipboards, reports.
> Clock in, clock out, coat and keys in hand.
> Lather, rinse, repeat.

Key in the door, I waltzed into the lounge like a woman possessed.

The dress.

I had to see her. Had to touch her, and let the echoes of the day's shift melt away. I spotted her, laying just as I had left her, gently strewn over the box of tissue she'd been sold in; sat on the armchair. I picked her up, held her aloft and brushed a small piece of lint off of her sleeve with a gentle smile. The material once again felt soothing; reassuring.

But now, I was struck with inspiration. And I knew what I had to do. It was no simple desire, no mere want. It was a need. An urge. And within an hour, I had pulled down the ladder for the attic, scrambled up through the trapdoor and begun my search.

I emerged triumphant, bearing the Singer. My old, faithful

sewing machine. Blowing the dust from its surfaces, I sat it down on the coffee table, and pulled the dress up and into the light. The dress was too plain, too shapeless. It was too much like the first petticoats I had swished in as a child. It just... wasn't quite me. Not yet.

I turned to face the second treasure I'd unearthed from storage – my old dress form. I was still the same size – a point of contention for some of my female friends, particularly those who had experienced motherhood – and I slid the dress over it, watching how it fell on this headless version of myself. The dress form was on wheels, and I span it around, looking at the drapery, and how it moved.

Is something missing? Perhaps a new neckline, or a new waist? Could I take it in... here? And here, maybe?

Pins in my mouth, consternation in my gaze, I began to work.

"Wow. That's... some dress."

I span gaily, removing my sunglasses. "You like it?"

"Yeah..." His dumbfounded silence overpowered his tongue. He struggled to find the words. "It's a right cracker. You look... stunning."

I gave a sheepish grin, and removed my headscarf. I had felt so glamorous when I left the house. It has been nearly three months, and my husband doesn't suspect a thing. But today, I was feeling particularly theatrical; had channelled Audrey and the spirit of Hollywood, and donned shades, a shawl and a little black dress to die for. Today I was no longer the timid little mouse, scurrying around the house trying not to disturb the man of the house, as he powered through coffees and business sections. I was no longer playing housewife, and the marigolds were off. I was sultry. I was daring. I was a vixen, off to meet my lover.

He extended his hand, his bedroom eyes full and inviting. I let the hotel door close behind me, and my fingers found his.

"I want you to take me."

Another night spent in the lounge.

This time, on waking, I didn't care to look at the clock. I had eyes only for the dress. Struggling to recall the exact alterations I had made yesterday afternoon, I was curious. What new glories would the morning bring?

My breath caught in my throat when I saw her. How she radiated sensuality. The sleeves had been removed, and looking closer, I could see they had been opened up and sewn together to create a kind of shrug, flung over the dress form's shoulders with a sense of debonair abandon. The waist had been cinched in, and the hem had been somehow altered to create the impression of multiple layers. Almost feathered.

She was beautiful. I loved her.

She reminded me of days when I had something to lose, but dared to gamble. Lines walked, crossed and left behind in the dust. Those two years, when I took a lover behind my husband's back. Illicit kisses in hotel rooms. An affair to remember.

I took the mannequin by the shoulders, and began to dance with her; leading her around the room in a ballroom waltz, as the memories washed over me.

It wasn't that my husband was passionless. But he was so subdued, and thought of me only as another possession in his house. And I remember, looking dowdy and frazzled in the supermarket one day, how another man approached me, after I knocked a bottle of olive oil off the shelf and was about three seconds away from bursting into tears.

He took my hand, tried to calm me down, and when a clerk found us, and radioed for a clean-up, he lied for me, and told them he'd dropped it. A small act of kindness in a moment of miniature disaster. It was silly, but my fingers still pricked with electricity. And the smell of olive oil has never been so intoxicatingly sweet.

After we'd paid for our goods, he took me to the supermarket cafe, and allowed me to buy him a coffee in thanks. And we talked good-naturedly, only a hint of flirtation beneath an otherwise innocent twenty minutes. He asked me if he could see me again, and I played nervously with my wedding ring. He seemed so genuine, so attractive, so… perceptive. But he never mentioned my husband.

We'd been sleeping together in hotel rooms, stealing moments when we could, for nearly six months, before he asked about him. Asked me why I didn't just leave him, if I was so unhappy. And I couldn't give him an answer. I didn't want to find the answer. Never even tried to reach for an excuse. I brushed him off with some empty turn of phrase, and he never asked again.

It was a time in life when I was happy. When I felt more like myself. More liberated, maybe. But not quite free. That wouldn't happen until much later, after the arguments at home grew more violent, more frequent, and more painful. But by then, the affair had died out. The bubbles disappeared until the champagne just ran flat. There was no dramatic moment – no ultimatum. He didn't find someone else, and I certainly didn't reignite my marriage. Sometimes things just… run out of steam.

At the office; the same routine.

> Briefings, charts and figures.
> Meetings, clipboards, reports.

Clock in, clock out, coat and keys in hand.
Lather, rinse, repeat.

I practically flew home. I had spent the last hour of my shift daydreaming about what changes I could make to her next. The progress I had made so far was good. Amazing, even. But it still wasn't me. It was someone who I used to be. A snapshot of a life gone by. And I was getting too old to spend my life wallowing in could-have-beens.

This dress was for me. It was not meant for anyone else – was not selected to impress any of the men in my life. Not for the three men I had loved – not my father, my secret lover, nor my ex-husband.

Just… me.

The sewing machine hummed to life when I touched it, and I emptied my handbag onto the coffee table, searching for the napkins I had scrawled designs on. My instruments of pleasure, lined in a row – scissors, a tape-measure, pins, ribbon, a small piece of elastic, a thimble, spare needles for the machine, extra thread.

These would aid my transformation.

I wanted out of the humdrum life. I wanted out of the endless parade of train stations, and grey suits, and meetings and reports, and nine-to-fives. The rat-race was slowly losing its charm, and my escape lay here. In this stretch of black material, in the delicate lines and folds and the soft, exhilarating caress of that fabric. I couldn't wait to finish it. Couldn't wait to place it on my body, after nearly three days of suspense. Good things came to those who wait. And I was tired of waiting.

I started work immediately. Needles danced in front of my eyes, and I barely stopped for breath, let alone food or coffee. I stopped, started, restarted, cursed and beamed – flicking between emotions and facial expressions as if they were television channels.

I was masquerading as a human who had a full range of emotions. I felt like nothing more than a doll. A mannequin which would bring this dress to life; and let her *breathe...*

"I guess that's it, then..."

The lawyers – sharks in tailored suits with white grins and sandpaper handshakes – had left the room. It wasn't a special room. Nothing extraordinary about it. A small aquarium in the background, it's filtration system providing a dull underscore to the silence.

He refused to answer. I couldn't tell whether it was because he was angry, upset, or numb. Not even the creases in the corners of his eyes gave him away. Not even a hint of how he might be feeling under the surface. In that moment, I longed to scratch away at the veneer of bravado; but it was futile. He wasn't my problem any more. Let someone else pick up the pieces.

I had come to the mediation meaning business I wanted our affairs put in order. I wanted my chains of bondage cut, and I wanted out. I was prepared to sacrifice all kinds of things – the wedding china, our pedigree dachshund, that weird blue vase that belonged in the hallway... All of it. Gone, and without regrets. All I wanted was my freedom.

Of course, my lawyer did all the dirty work, pulling at his leash, and growling and nipping in all the right places, until I had enough financial stability, and everything was deemed fair. A fairly amicable division of assets, apparently.

In the boardroom, I sat, wearing a bright red dress. It was sleeveless and strapless, and showed more cleavage than I usually dared. It had a peplum waist, unlike anything else I owned; and I paired it with some widow-maker heels, and a gash of scarlet lipstick. I watched my soon-to-be-ex-husband with a fixed gaze throughout. And I didn't say a word. Not until after.

"I guess that's it, then..."

He eventually looked up, as if seeing me for the first time that day.

He cleared his throat, then his eyes glazed over; as if he were remembering the first time he ever saw me. A pause. And, eventually... "You look nice. That's a cracker of a dress. You certainly mean business today, don't you?"

I gave him a small, sad smile. I had been prepared to lose a lot, but he'd come off significantly worse. I had taken him to the proverbial cleaners, and now I was free. I didn't have to answer to clicked fingers any more.

"Thank you for the lovely marriage. I had a nice time."

And with that, I span on my heel, and sashayed out of the offices, feeling eyes on my legs and thighs and swaying hips every strutted step of the way.

Somehow, I had gotten lost. Lost among deadlines and thankless tasks. Buried under train timetables, and clocking-in cards, and receipts for designer coffees and deli-counter sandwiches. My life had become so... drab. So normal. In a word... boring.

I had cheated to escape my marriage. But in the end, I was so much happier alone. And I still am. I just need to find the right things to fill my life with. The right moments to get lost in. The right objects to bury myself in.

And right now, it's the old Singer. This dress-form. And the dress. I can't explain this compulsion, but as I lay here, on the sofa, wearing only this beautiful creation... No straps, no sleeves; just a tightly hugging black form, with a peplum and all the markings of both a 'come-fuck-me' and a 'go-fuck-yourself' outfit...

82

The excess material is bunched over my legs like a makeshift quilt. And as I stretched, and yawned, it stroked my legs in vivid flashes. Like a lover's hand. And so I let it guide my own. Across the folds of the dress, across the folds of my own skin. I wasn't sure where either started or ended now.

In this moment, I was a doll, a woman, a dress-form and the dress. And I was a sea of hands; enquiring fingers; delicate mouths.

And so I lay there, nestled amongst the kisses and touches of hundreds of concubines. And every one was made of black velveteen, and every one made me shudder as its fingers crept oh so slowly up my thigh...

...and it's softer than I thought it would be.

Softer, yet, somehow... heavier.

About the author

Christopher Bowles has previously appeared in several Bridge House anthologies, including *Snowflakes*, *Baubles* and *Glit-er-ary Tales*. His fable *The Virtuous Farmer* was also selected as a winner of the 2018 Waterloo Writing Festival, appearing in their *To Be... To Become* e-collection.

Last year saw the launch of his first single-author flash-fiction collection, *Spectrum,* with an accompanying solo spoken word show; which he is currently adapting into an audiobook.

Eton Mess

Merlin Ward

A self-fulfilling prophesy

It was a non-smoking carriage but the skinhead couldn't read the sign or, maybe it was he didn't care. Keen to get off the train, the young actor slid down the window, turned the handle and, making sure he didn't hit anyone standing on the platform, he opened the door, jumping off whilst the train was still entering Charing Cross Station. He handed in his ticket to the inspector at the gate and checked the time on his Longines watch, a gift from his parents. "Peter," said his father handing his son the velvet covered box. "Time is short. Use it wisely."

Peter headed out of the grimy station, walking quickly past some kids with a transistor radio that was blaring out his favourite T. Rex song 'Ride a White Swan'. Marc Bolan was the glam rock star of 1971. It was also a good year for Peter who was playing a major role in his third West End play at the tender age of nineteen.

Life was good; he had money, a burgeoning acting career, and an exciting evening in prospect. He'd been invited to help out at a showbiz party for the princely sum of £10; not just any showbiz party but one given by the UK's leading playwright.

"Here you are, dearie." Lavender wrapped in tin foil was shoved under his nose, by a woman, with a lined, sun-hardened face. "For luck," she said.

"Thank you." He took the tiny bunch and with a smile headed off.

"Well, give us something for it!" shouted the woman, running after him.

The actor turned and handed back the lavender. "I thought it was a gift. I don't have any spare money." He hurried away.

"Then a curse will be upon you. Bad luck will dog your footsteps wherever you may go."

The old crone was clearly bonkers and he laughed at the threat as he hurried to the underground station on the corner of Trafalgar Square. As he ran down the stairs it felt a bit strange to be going to a party on a Sunday evening, but it is the only night of the week when actors working in the theatre are free to go out.

The house in Tregunter Road was enormous by London standards. The playwright's wife, Amanda, opened the door and showed him through to the kitchen where he was introduced to Charles. Peter felt his heart pounding in such esteemed company but was put at ease when the playwright opened a giant-sized fridge, stuffed with bottles of Champagne.

"This is what we're serving. The glasses are over there. Make sure everyone is looked after and then join the party. Feel free to have a good time; mix, circulate."

A little girl ran into the kitchen and announced to the actor that dinner was to be served downstairs. "But I have to go to bed and it's not fair!"

"It's going to be a bit crowded in the basement," explained the playwright's wife. "But we should just about seat everyone. I may need your help serving the food."

The doorbell rang.

Peter went to open the front door and the first guests arrived. He didn't recognise the American and his wife but his interest was sparked when Charles introduced Peter to the Hollywood producer who was turning his hit play into a major movie. From that moment on the actor's role was to open the front door, take any coats and serve Champagne to the continuing flow of famous faces.

The party was in full swing when the playwright came into the kitchen. "We have a couple of late arrivals. Could you do the honours?" The excited actor poured two Champagne flutes and took them into the main reception room where the atmosphere was truly buzzing. He looked around the guests through all their cigarette smoke and then he saw them – crystal blue eyes, sparkling from a stunningly beautiful face, complemented by curling blonde hair. The Hollywood star turned her perfect pools of blue towards him and he fell in love. He gave her a glass of Champagne, completely ignoring the man standing beside her.

"Are you an actor?" Miss Remick was talking to him! Life could not get any better. Somehow, he found the words to reply and blurted out how much he loved her work.

"I think that's for me." Peter looked at her husband for the first time.

"Oh, yes, of course." Embarrassed, he handed over the glass of Champagne and backed away.

The guests were ushered down to the basement, which was decked out like a bistro. Every now and then, the young actor would steal a glance at the vibrant blue eyes. She was surrounded by famous faces all vying for her attention and he made the regular promise to himself that he too would be famous one day.

"Peter, we've run out of plates. Could you get those displayed on the dresser?" Amanda indicated a pine Welsh Dresser on the far side of the improvised bistro. Getting the plates was not an easy task as there was not much room between the chairs. Fortunately, Peter's thirty inch waist served him well and with a few apologies he made it back without disturbing too many film stars.

Eton Mess was new to Peter but it looked good – chopped strawberries whipped with cream, with meringues stirred in and raspberry juice poured over the finished result. Taking great care, the actor performed like a waiter at the Ritz as he served the animated guests.

The Hollywood film producer was in deep conversation with Miss Remick as Peter eased his way behind his chair, holding two great piles of Eton Mess high above the man's balding head. Without warning, one of the plates broke apart and crockery followed by raspberry juice, whipped strawberry cream and meringue, splattered onto the powerful man's head and down his neck.

The producer leapt to his feet with a cry as bits of porcelain clattered onto the tiled floor. Every pair of famous eyes in the room turned towards the young actor who was holding a section of plate.

"It just disintegrated!" Peter announced to his celebrated audience.

His feeble excuse brought the house down and everyone burst out laughing. Blushing as red as raspberry juice, Peter tried to help the producer clean up, but he was roughly pushed away.

The playwright's wife came to the actor's aid and she and the crystal blue eyes wiped away the mess as best they could with numerous proffered napkins. Later, Amanda explained to the distressed young man that the plate had been broken a few years back and the pieces stuck together.

"The weight of the food must have been too much for the UHU," added the amused playwright.

Peter begged his hosts to make an announcement; to tell the famous people and especially Miss Remick that the accident was not his fault. Charles laughed and said it was a brilliant climax to the evening and that the young actor should not worry. To make up for the embarrassment he gave him double the agreed fee. But money could never make up for the humiliation the teenager felt. His career in movies was doomed before it had even begun. He left for home with a full wallet and an empty heart, unaware that the Eton Mess had stained his white shirt blood red.

At Charing Cross railway station, a police constable grabbed the despondent young man.

"What's happened to you, sonny? Is that your blood?"

"No"

"Someone else's, then?"

"It's raspberry juice. Eton Mess. I had an accident at a showbiz party."

The policeman laughed and let him go. "You an actor, then?"

"Yes."

"Famous?"

"I hope to be. I'm in a play at the moment."

"Theatre? You want to get into the flicks, young man."

His train was leaving for Sevenoaks in ten minutes, enough time to do what he knew he had to do. Where was she? Where was the gypsy woman with the hard face and the broken-toothed smile? It was a relief when he spotted her.

She saw him coming. He looked wounded and dangerous. She felt for a slim blade and eased it into her hand as the young man reached inside his jacket. What for? A knife? A gun? She was too long in the tooth to be caught out by a callow youth. Her target was the red circle bleeding down his shirt.

Peter felt for one of the ten pound notes he'd been given as he approached the woman. He was determined to buy her good wishes and, hopefully, for the curse to be undone.

There was no resistance to the razor-sharp blade. The actor's hand shot out from his jacket gripping the ten pound note, which the gypsy extracted from his fingers as she pulled the blade out of his flesh. She turned away as the young man fell to his knees, fresh blood mingling with the Eton Mess.

He knew he was hurt but he had to catch the last train home. He got to his feet and staggered towards the ticket barrier. The inspector saw the young man with the spreading red stain and rushed to his aid but the policeman brought him up short.

"Leave him. He's an actor. It's just some raspberry juice. Alas poor Yorick and all that."

The wounded teenager managed to get on the train and sat down in a corner seat opposite another young skinhead. Several doors slammed shut; the guard blew a shrill blast on his whistle and the train pulled out of the station.

At Orpington, the skinhead felt good as he leapt off the train onto the platform. He was ten pounds richer and the proud owner of a lovely Swiss, Longines watch.

The actor did not get off at Sevenoaks but travelled all the way to the end of the line.

The following night, a young understudy got his big break when he stepped, for the first time onto a West End stage in front of a packed house.

About the author
At the age of sixteen, Merlin Ward entered the theatre in Alan Bennett's first play, *Forty Years On*. He continued working on the West End stage and also on TV, becoming a well-known face when he played Dennis Harper, a Cockney garage mechanic, in the soap, *Crossroads*. Always keen on writing, he wrote the screenplay for the film *Out of Bound*, which he also directed. Set in a girls' boarding school, the film has screened three times on BBC One. More recently, Merlin has written for the stage, and his play *The Widow*, a supernatural thriller, has been performed in the UK and USA.

www.merlinward.co.uk

Firecracker

Elizabeth Cox

Thud! The missile hit the ground by her left foot causing
Marilee to grab her flowing skirt. Crack! She jumped, as it
exploded leaving a faint smell of burning in the air. Startled,
a screeching parrot fluttered over her head its blue wings
almost touching her hair. She ducked. A whining sound
filled the air. A firecracker! It whirled around her dropping
at her feet, its red eye glowing in a sinister fashion. Her
instinct was to flee. Hoisting her blue silk sarong around
her waist, she tucked it in tightly exposing her diamante
sandals and long brown legs, as she took flight.

"Where you goin' Marilee?" a man's voice came from
nowhere, echoing around the jungle clearing. Marilee
stopped. It was a strange voice, deep yet splintered.

"Who's there?" She sounded timid, but she couldn't
deny she was scared. "Who's there? Show yourself. Only
people with something to hide creep about frightening folks
to death. Did you throw that thing?" Her words strung
themselves around the creepers like pearls on her
grandma's necklace.

"You scared Marilee?" Swinging around in the
direction of the voice which now seemed closer, she could
see nothing in the twilight under the tree canopy. In the
distance she could hear the comforting elemental beat of the
drum leading the carnival parade. Today was carnival in her
town. Guitars and horns started up in harmony; the familiar
music made her smile despite herself. She loved the
carnival.

"Who is it? Stop messing about and show yourself. Is it
you Petey? You're daft enough to pull a stunt like this." Her
friend Petey was always playing tricks on her. She clutched

her arms around her body, aware that she was shivering even though the evening was warm. She knew she should run, but her feet had planted themselves firmly in the soft leaf-mould of the forest floor as if they had taken root. There was a soft thwack, as something fell to earth alongside her. She screamed. A hollow laugh rang out across the silence.

"Did I scare you, Marilee? Sorry about that." The voice was louder now and seemed to be moving towards her.

"Stop it! What have I ever done to you?" The happy sounds of the carnival revellers rumbled around the damask night. Shouts and laughter, laughter and shouting. Music and joy. Far away. Something rustled in the undergrowth, and she jumped, her heart beating wildly. A brown mouse scampered across the clearing. She sighed with relief, until she heard the rustling again much closer now. It could be a wild cat or even a tiger. *'Tyger Tyger… burning bright… in the forests of the night'*. Reciting her favourite poem from her school days, she hoped it would bring her comfort or even make the invisible tiger feel kindly towards her. Don't be stupid, she told herself, there haven't been tigers around here for ages. Anyway, tigers don't speak. Do they? A cool breeze fluttered the leaves on the nearby tree. She swung around sharply. Nothing to be seen. Except, there on floor glowing softly by her foot was another firecracker.

"Hi Marilee, did you think I'd gone away?" The treacly voice was very close now. Marilee peered into the undergrowth in vain. The blaring of the carnival trumpets now seemed miles away; the notes carrying on the soft warm breeze towards her. The parade must be around the other side of the town. Soon people would be gathering in the square, and the dancing would begin. She loved dancing and began swaying to the happy sounds. The barbecue fires had been lit. Wood-smoke filled the night mingling with the intense scent of Frangipani flowers and earthy loam, damp after a rainstorm. Soon the pork would be turning on the spit. It made her happy for a moment. Marilee wished she was back in the town along with her friends. They would be enjoying the music and dancing, eating the newly cooked spicy meat and singing their hearts out.

Marilee glanced down at the object lying near her foot. The little red eye glowed sharply then died away. She gathered all her courage and pushed it with her toe. It rolled over.

"It won't hurt you, Marilee," the voice rang out. It was behind her now. She swivelled on her heel. All she could see were the ghostly white flowers of the Frangipani glowing like moons against the dense green of the undergrowth. Like the pale eyes of phantom cats.

As the raucous sounds of the carnival grew louder, the delicious aroma of the cooking food penetrated deeper into the thick undergrowth, and her stomach growled. Her little sister and brother would be enjoying the roasted corn and pork crackling, trailing around the stalls holding tightly onto Mama and Papa's hands. She should never have come to the forest. Her mission to collect flowers to make the best carnival headdress was long forgotten.

"Smells good doesn't it, Marilee. You're missing out. Shame you're stuck here in the forest with me." At that moment another of the red eyed firecrackers fell by her feet. She gasped holding her body stiff. It glowed and fizzed. She shuffled towards the other side of the clearing, moving each foot an inch at a time.

"Who are you?" she whispered, her voice breaking a little. "What do you want with me?"

"I'm your friend, Marilee, I'm here to look after you. Keep you from harm in the forest. You can't be too careful." The sound of his voice was creeping closer to where she was standing. Her hands were shaking, as she defied the silky voice.

"Show yourself, if I've nothing to fear from you." Another of the red eyed fireworks landed at her feet. "Stop it. Just stop it. Show yourself," she shouted in the direction of the missile's trajectory. "Stop throwing those things. It's getting annoying now." She stamped her foot on the stick and the red eye died, sending sparks in every direction. The branches of the ferns swayed, although there was no breeze. She clutched her throat.

"Is that you, Petey? Stop playing tricks. That's enough now." Fear tightened her throat, transforming her voice into a nervous squeak. The branches rustled again. She peered into the darkness seeking the glow of a tiger's eyes. Nothing. She breathed a sigh of relief, until another stick landed by her right foot and exploded with a loud "Crack!" She stamped on it again and again, until it was flattened, the red paper ripped to shreds. "There! That serves you right," she screamed, "you can't frighten me."

"Oh! Marilee, you shouldn't have done that. I'll have to send another one." The voice was angry now and louder, closer.

"Do what you like, I don't care," she called out, "I'm going to pick some Frangipani to make my carnival headdress, and then I'm leaving."

"I can't let you go, Marilee. You came here, you've got to stay here now," the voice murmured.

"Well show yourself then, let me see you. I haven't got time to waste. I need to get back to the carnival, before all the food is gone. Mama will be expecting me soon." The soft air of the tropical night enclosed her, as she moved towards the Frangipani trees. Her fear was forgotten in the joy of gently breaking the blossoms from the branches, careful to avoid the poisonous sap from coating her fingers. The scent was wondrous. Nothing could hurt her on such a

93

night, could it? She sang to herself as she picked, happy songs, sad songs, new songs, old songs. Then soft footsteps sounded behind her muffled by the leaf-strewn forest floor. A slow dragging sound punctuated by snapping twigs.

"I'm here, Marilee." Frightened to turn around, she stayed facing the trees gripping tightly onto her bouquet of flowers, her knuckles white. "Turn around." Above the silence of the glade, the brassy notes of the trumpets blared out. People could be heard laughing and shouting with joy. They seemed a world away now. How she wished she were there. Her feet were like stones planted deep into the ground. An ant ran over her sandal catching itself in the diamante of the strap. She watched it, as it struggled to get free. It finally gave up the struggle and was still. She felt a slight movement in the air current, as someone moved closer to her. Warm breath touched the back of her neck above the orange silk of her bodice and below her hairline. She shuddered, as she felt rough fingers loosen the flowers from her hair letting it fall down her back. The hand moved to her shoulder and slowly turned her around. She was as helpless, as if she were a puppet. Then she was looking into the eyes of her tormenter. It wasn't her friend Petey.

"Hello, Marilee. I told you I wouldn't let you leave me. I need you here in the forest."

Marilee lifted her head to look into a pair of green eyes, the same colour as the forest plants. The hand resting on her shoulder was slender, the skin a soft shade of coffee with nails which tapered into sharp points. They did not hurt her. The man's hair was black and thick falling to his waist. In his other hand he held a bunch of firecrackers.

"I'm sorry about the firecrackers, but I had to gain your attention. You are the one I have chosen to live with me in the forest." His insidious voice rang out around the glade.

Marilee scanned the man's face which was strong yet

gentle, his mouth generous. His wide smile lit up the forest. A fern green sarong was swathed around his strong body and grazed his bare feet. He only had four toes on each foot; the first and second fused together.

"Who are you, why do you want me to stay with you? What do you mean?" She was scared yet mesmerized by his flickering eyes which changed colour constantly from green to blue. She could not look away. "Why did you try to frighten me? I can't stay here with you. My mama is waiting for me at the carnival, I must go. They may even be coming to look for me." Marilee pulled away from him, but he gripped her shoulder with his talons. She tried to shake him off. "Let go, I need to leave!" Her voice faltered the more she tried to break free.

"Marilee, every time you come into the forest I'm there close to you. I'm the breeze on the leaves, the rustle in the grass, the shadowy figure in the undergrowth."

"You're insane." Marilee had now stopped struggling and faced him. "I'm going now, don't try to stop me." She turned to run out of the clearing, but he appeared in front of her barring her way.

"No Marilee, I'm not insane. I love you." He held her gaze and took her hand. "Come with me, please."

"Don't be silly. How can you love me we've never met before?"

Marilee was beginning to think this was all a little surreal and couldn't get away fast enough. She tried to shake her hand free, but he held it tighter.

"Oh, Marilee, you're very unkind to me. All I want is to show you my home deep in the forest. Then you can see I'm not going to hurt you." Marilee was not sure, but perhaps if she allowed him to show her, he would let her go back. He didn't look very scary, except for his glittering eyes and his nails of course.

95

"Just for a minute then," she said, "my family will be looking for me, it's late." She allowed him to take her hand and lead her into the depths of the forest. The canopy closed around them and silence fell on the glade.

"Marilee! Marilee! Where are you? We've been looking for you for ages, you're missing all the fun of the carnival." Her mama and papa entered the clearing holding hands with her brother Marius and sister Dolores. Dolores broke free from her papa's hand.

"Look Mama, there's Marilee's scarf over there, the blue one which goes with her best sarong," shouted Dolores as she ran to pick it up and pressed it close to her face, before handing it to her mother. "She must be here somewhere. Ooh! Look at all these firecrackers on the floor, Mama. I bet she and Petey had lots of fun." Her voice was full of envy. The little girl kicked them around with her foot. Marius ran to join her.

"That boy's never up to any good," her mother remonstrated impatiently, her opinion of Petey without doubt. Mama stuffed the abandoned scarf in her pocket, "Careless girl! Well they're certainly not here. They must have returned to the carnival by the other path. We'll find her back in the square I expect."

Mama and Papa and the children left the clearing following the path through the trees back to the festivities. Silent eyes watched them from the undergrowth, as they left.

About the author

Elizabeth lives on Anglesey. She spends her time working at the 'day job' and writing short stories, poetry and attempting to finish her first novel. Her short story, *Winking at Angels*, was published in the *Baubles* anthology in 2016, and *A Little Bit of Sparkle* was published in *Glit-er-ary* in 2017. When inspiration dries up, she gazes at the wonderful Snowdon mountain range from her window until it returns.

Horseflesh

Adrian Naylor

1.

I feel I should start with something dramatic: as I sit here, unsure who will read this in the months and years to come I feel a weight of responsibility. And yet as I look around me I see normal everyday objects and surroundings. Is history always so humdrum?

I suppose it started with the Bolognese. Who'd have dreamt the beginning of the end would be a value ready-meal? Although the poetry of the justice does make you laugh. But I won't start there – not yet. I have a little time, if not enough.

2.

My name is Craig Kennedy and I was that fat, pasty kid at school with the unhealthy interest in science. I was born in Wolverhampton, England, into working-class suburbia with two older brothers, a fussy mother and a dad who got laid off from Rover when I was only eight. It was just before Christmas – wonderful sense of timing – and I'd wanted a microscope. Only Santa sent his apologies and a Subbuteo set instead.

I finally got the microscope three Christmases later – Dad was working at a garage and Mum had gone part-time at the Co-op. I remember opening the box, remember the feel of the cloth lining, and of the deliciously cold metal.

"Make sure you don't break it!" Mum shouted – as if I would break the most fabulous, fantastical object in the whole wide world. I was fascinated by anything small – especially anything small and alive. Would you believe I have a tear in my eye? It's been happening a lot lately. Been thinking too much – not much else to do. If I do go off on a tangent please bear with me – I usually overcompensate with humour but I'm not sure I've much of that left.

3.

I studied biology at Nottingham and got a Desmond (that's a Desmond Tutu – a 2:2, lower second. Think 'grade C') for my troubles. Mum was chuffed to little mint balls. It was difficult to tell with Dad – he was the quiet, buttoned-up sort – but I think he was proud. I was the first in the family to get a degree: they stood in Sunday-best for graduation looking as uncomfortable as I felt in that stupid gown and hat. We ate at a local Harvester and I had gammon and chips. Mum's happiness contrasted with her normal doom and gloom – nowadays she'd probably be diagnosed as bipolar but then it was just 'moody'. When this all started it was her who first decided it was the end of the world, her who'd read the prophecies in the Daily Mail. 'Mayan' this, and 'cataclysm' that.

Dear God! I thought then.

Dear God, I think now.

What do you want to be when you grow up, they ask kids. What do kids know? By the time the kid knows the answers aren't as interesting. Everyone wants to talk about being a spaceman or a footballer; few are interested in bank clerks or research analysts.

That last one? Yep: that's me. They say you should do what you enjoy. And in my case they were right: I like studying small stuff – simple as that. I wound up with a largish research company and one day I'd be analysing drugs for some pharmaceutical giant, the next testing it for the government body charged with regulating them. Or even some protest group determined to prove it's the cause of death and deformity. The irony!

4.

Mum phoned the day the news broke – seems they'd found horsemeat in some Findus cheapy value-meal.

"I've been saying this for years!" she triumphed. "You can't tell what's in that stuff! They use all sorts..." And proceeded to tell me all about it.

"And have you eaten any?" I asked innocently.

"Cheeky sod!" she said. "You saying I'm a horse?" How on earth she got from A to B I'm not sure but she took umbrage (sorry, that means offence). Once she'd calmed down it turned out that she had, and there was more in the freezer.

"I'm not wasting them, mind – I bet there's ten pounds worth in there!"

Of course that was just the start. First it was Tesco then Aldi, a few days later Sainsbury's and Asda too. Government and the Food Standards Agency were on the news from day one pointing the finger: first at organised crime syndicates then, even better: *foreign* organised crime syndicates. Romanians! Great: more to fan the flames of Daily Mail intolerance. Then it was local councils demanding cheaper meat for schools! But I'm not here to pontificate. All I know is it was brewing nicely.

And speaking of pontification, it was then that the Pope resigned.

5.

Now you might not see the connection – I certainly didn't – and in one obvious sense there isn't. Yet strangely it turned out that there was.

"End of the world," said Mum matter-of-factly a few days later. I'd been hard at it all week – must have been a Friday come to think of it – with all the testing. We had the contract, or *a* contract, from the FSA. They'd shipped shed-loads of processed meat into out fridges and it was like a production line. The balloon had gone up big-time. Of course they expected to find that the horsemeat was only in products from certain (foreign!) locations. But what happened was that they found it absolutely everywhere. Me and Tony (Oates) found it hugely amusing. Don't get me wrong, an utter crime, but it's only horsemeat, right? And I'd seen a lot worse. Well, I had up till that point.

Anyway, the point is this scandal suddenly got huge. I'd been run off my feet, worked till midnight for three nights running, arrived home with a takeaway curry and there's Mum with news of The Apocalypse.

"The prophecies say the end will come two Popes after John Paul the Second!"

"So?" I asked through a mouthful of Lamb Rogan while watching *Wheeler-dealers*: who says men can't multi-task?

"Well the *next* one is *him!* And then there's this meteor business."

"Oh yes?" I was in auto-response mode: sometimes it's the only way to survive.

"In Russia. Fireballs from the sky…!"

"Sorry – what?"

6.

You probably remember the meteor if only because of the camera-phone footage of it streaking across the sky. I'd seen none of it, having spent the week in a lab or on the Tube. I'd barely seen daylight let alone TV.

"It's a sign!"

"It is *not* a sign, Mother, it's just happenstance. Anyway it didn't hit anyone, did it?"

"That's not the point! It's an *omen* – it's the plagues to come that'll cause the weeping and wailing and gnashing of teeth!" She was saying it for effect. "First the Pope, now the meteor. And the food contamination!"

"It's not contaminated; remember I test it for a living, it's perfectly fine..."

"It *is* contaminated – it's contaminated with horse..."

"But that's not..."

"...and heaven knows what else!" Sometimes you just don't argue.

"How's Dad?"

7.

Sorry about the gap: it's now Sunday morning. Only I suppose you didn't notice, did you? Got distracted, went to check the traps then fell asleep. I seem to be doing that a lot lately.

Just re-read what I've written and realise how far off the point I've wandered. I guess I've been finding it therapeutic – is that how you spell it? Spelling's just one of the things that doesn't matter anymore. What's the song? 'You don't know what you've got till it's gone'? Then something about a parking lot that I never understood.

Got an email from the Nigerian Prime Minister this morning! 'We would like to deposit fifty million dollars...' etc. Made me laugh. Are people actually still out there sending this stuff? It must be machines, still churning it out even after the people have gone. Free spins, your PPI claim has been successful and you may be entitled to a bigger penis. Funny to think when they sent that spacecraft off looking for aliens in the seventies they thought long and hard what message to put on it to explain who the human race were. Now all this crap is being sent out automatically and it's *that* which will tell the little green men who we were.

Were.

8.

Like I say we work for all kinds of organisations but the main work is government stuff – a blue label always takes priority. Sometimes I don't know what it is I'm testing for, though I'm smart enough to make a good guess. There's poisons and toxins and all sorts of grim stuff. Conscience? If I didn't do it someone else would. A thin defence I know but let he who is without sin etc. Been reading a lot of The Bible lately.

So Craddock brings in a load of big-wigs – up in the conference room I only ever get invited to on special occasions. There's glasses and water but no food – a bad sign.

"Ah, Mr Kennedy, sit down," Mister – another bad sign. "I'm Kevin Wilson, this is Mr Telling and Mr Tabbard. We need your help." My help: fabulous! Dodgy, I thought, but fabulous. "This horsemeat business – as you know it's worse than we thought. Everyone's at it, which in some ways makes it better than a limited scale event."

"For us," added Mr Tabbard – a wiry man with a moustache and no discernible personality.

"Indeed," confirmed Kevin Wilson. Long story short – they had a mountain of testing needed doing in secret. Wanted to know more about the horses: were they diseased, was there a common source, and was there anything else in there.

"So basically if there's more bad news, you want me to find it first?"

"Exactly."

"So no one else does."

The third man, Telling, smiled a measured smile. That's how I recall it – *measured.*

"I won't tell you otherwise, Mr Kennedy. Yes – we need to know and we need others not to. And we need to know fast."

And that's how I ended up working two weeks of lates with Tony Oakes – a man I would not trust with my pet rabbit and Rob Brinkley, quite possibly the world's dullest individual.

9.

In my head this was a simple story – it was going to take me half an hour at most. Power's fine for the moment by the way – don't know if that's something else that's on automatic. Not sure what I'll do when – *if* – it fails. Don't want to think about that.

10.

We broke the samples down by product, date and source location. There were ready-meals, mince and cooked stuff like sausage rolls and pasties. We had cling-filmed school dinners in huge aluminium trays and vats from hospitals and homes. In the first few days we nearly gave up, we were getting through it at a tenth the rate it was arriving, but once we got up and running the results on the spread-sheets grew.

The first thing we tested was the horse DNA. Find the origin, they said. Not so easy. Oakes and me ran some comparisons – all from scratch of course. 'Always from first principles, Mr Kennedy. *Empirical empirical*

empirical!' (Professor Davies: terrible BO). Meanwhile Brinkley boned up on existing research. We have access to all sorts of stuff: you really would not believe the papers people write. Anyway, off we go logging all this data, updating Craddock twice a day. By Friday we had enough data to start plotting and sure enough it's looking like there's a limited number of sources – breeds, I mean.

Now this wasn't surprising – if this was a wide-scale operation common sources, cheaper breeds could be expected. This wasn't the odd old nag or faller at the first at Ascot; this was horsemeat on an industrial scale.

Now Craddock is an arse, and rather than congratulate us he just moans.

"What about disease – this tells me nothing about disease!" We need to work systematically, I say, get the basics out of the way first, but he just goes on and on. That was just before the weekend Mum went off on her 'here comes The Apocalypse' phone call. You can see why I wasn't in the mood.

11.

The following week it started getting really weird. We were studying DNA patterns up on an interactive screen – well, me and Brinkley were: Oates was on You Tube.

"There's four groups," said Brinkley.

"Four breeds – any ideas what?"

"Got a list of major horsemeat sources here," another set of bars appeared overlaying the test results. You've seen DNA diagrams: stacks of horizontal lines and gaps; looks like when you de-frag your hard-drive. Problem number one: "They don't match." That was obvious but needed saying: none of our samples was anywhere close to the 'normal' sources.

"Eh?" Oates looked up, Mars-bar protruding obscenely from his mouth.

"They must have some new breed out there in Romania."

"Okay but it must be related to an existing breed, Brinks," I said, "Show us some more breeds – can't be difficult to narrow it down."

"There's quite a few," said Brinkley in his dull monotone. "Best let Monica chew through them." Monica was Brinkley's DNA analysis software. We called it Mrs Brinkley.

So what did Monica find?

"Gentlemen, I suggest you sit down for this," announced Brinkley, grandly. He had a habit of announcing things grandly so at first we didn't bother. It was the following morning – Thursday, I think. Oates and me had had a late-night session in the Parrot and Starfish. We were tired, bored and slightly hung-over.

"Just tell us, Brinks."

"No, I mean it – sit down." This sounded unusually forceful and Oates looked at me and I looked at Oakes and we both sat down.

"Okay so first we thank Monica for cleverly coming up with three things we didn't know before." Silence. "Guys – you know the rules: thank Monica for all the work she's just saved us."

I think I mumbled something rude.

"Okay. So firstly our samples are none of the usual breeds."

"We knew that."

"No, we suspected that, Craigie. *Now* we know it." Oates and me did that 'exchanged glances' thing. "Second – we have no match for the breed against *any* breed of horse on the record…"

105

"Great – another duff database…" began Oates.

"Far from it – this database contains every single horse breed ever discovered."

"Sorry – are you saying we've just discovered a new breed of horse?"

"We haven't – someone out in Romania has," I replied. "And they're chopping them up and eating them."

Brinkley frowned.

"Is that likely?"

"That someone's bred an edible horse? Possibly – we pretty much did that with cows and pigs in the seventeenth and eighteenth centuries."

"No no no. If you purpose-bred them they'd at least resemble whatever they were based on – no matter how different they looked."

Silence.

"Three – you said Monica had found out three things?"

"Oh yes – whatever breed or breeds they are, and maybe this isn't such a surprise, they are extremely interbred. The DNA within each group is almost identical."

Almost.

12.

We agreed to carry on testing and didn't mention what we'd found to Craddock. In the meantime the net widened: we tested kebabs and dripping and just about everything in between. Only a fraction hit the papers and the requests for updates were increasing. As were those from Mum.

"What's going on, Craig? You must know about this horsemeat business."

"Well…" I started, but she continued anyway.

"Mrs Rogers agrees it's a sign. First the Pope, then this, and the meteor. Well…" I wasn't sure how the meteor was

106

connected but in her head these things went together like apple-pie and custard.

Next day was Friday. I was meant to go to Bristol to visit Lianne but of course I never got there. Just before the Friday afternoon briefing we got results back which stunned us into telling Craddock.

"No diseases yet?"

"No diseases," I replied.

"What about origin, what can you tell me?"

Oates ran his hand through his hair and looked at me. I shrugged back: weird or not it was time he knew.

"Right – well it's like this. We narrowed it down to four breeds of horse – or at least we thought they were breeds."

"Which ones?"

"Well that's the odd thing – they aren't on the database," said Oates. He liked being the spokesman.

"Shit – you mean we've bought crap data again?"

"No no, you don't understand: they are *no, known* breed. They're new: unique."

"A new breed of horse? Seriously?" said Craddock, looking from one to the other.

"It's not as simple as that. There's four kinds of horse – all very distinct, and all very unlike anything anyone's seen before," said Oates, warming to the task of doom-monger.

"And?"

"And the punchline is – we just re-analysed their DNA and we found a calibration error. We knew we had a narrow pool with abnormally similar DNA which we put down to excessive interbreeding…"

"Great: first mad cows, now mad horses!"

"Not mad horses, Mr Craddock: mad *horse*. We've analysed meat taken from across the EU, huge volumes. We're talking massive quantities here. But the recalibrated results show that the DNA isn't just very similar, it's utterly

107

identical. Each group isn't a breed – it's a, single solitary horse."

13.

I may have made some of that up for dramatic effect, but I don't think so. But then I've been imagining other stuff recently, so who knows?

I checked the traps again: nothing. No email either. There look to be people out there – not everyone was affected. But can I trust them? Even if I meet someone who's infected I still have a three in four chance of being okay: but what if I meet the fourth type? I've see the pictures.

14.

So we did what any normal, reasonable human beings would do when struck with the inexplicable – we went down the pub. It seems amazing to me now that we spent that night like any other. The Parrot and Starfish was rocking, and the horsemeat jokes were rife. Did you know that Hamburgers is an anagram of Shergar Bum? We got to theorising, me and Oates (Brinkley had cried off, ill).

Just four horses. That fact rattled round inside my head all night. We won on the quiz machine for the first time ever! The link is that I Googled something when I got home checked some answer. Must have been one or two in the morning. I was half-cut – spilled coffee all over my iPad. I was about to go to bed when I decided to Google something else. I'd like to say 'then it hit me' but it didn't, not immediately. Because what I found didn't seem to have anything to do with our tests. In my head I'd drawn a blank.

Some blank.

15.

Brinkley was a no-show Saturday; we'd decided to work the afternoon to dig into some new arrivals, frankly we were hoping to find something that disproved our hypothesis. We had the footy on the radio: QPR had just scored and Oates was out for a pee.

I told you about my microscope fetish. You don't use them for DNA that's all high-tech microanalysis gear. But I was curious to see our four horses close up. It's a biologist's thing: we have to see things in detail, to see movement, life. Then we understand.

We'd nicknamed the four groups Tom, Dick, Harry and Jane. There was no pattern to where they'd been found – all four had turned up in the UK, the last three also in France and Germany, the first and third in Italy. I started with Tom.

On low magnification everything looked fine: just dead tissue cells, nothing untoward. Then I turned up the resolution. The power was incredible – that first one I got as a kid was maybe a hundred times: this was *eighteen-*hundred. I looked at Tom again and still nothing: all quiet. I thought the same of Dick at first but then I noticed something odd: the cell was moving slightly. Now this thing was dead remember, dead dead dead. But it moved! Then suddenly one cell pushed against another and 'pop' – the two merged! This is *not* what dead cells do. It was alive – and destructive. I looked back at the slide with Tom on it – it wasn't doing the same. I moved on to Harry. Nothing. QPR got a second; Oates noisily sat down at his desk. I blinked: one of Harry's cells seemed to have got smaller. The scope's got a record function: I looked up and played it back.

"Oates! Look at this!" He strolled over.

"Bloody hell – that's odd."

16.

I recorded each sample over a thirty-minute period.

"We won't find out what this is all about you know," moaned Oates. "It'll just get interesting when they'll whisk the results off somewhere and we'll get reminded of our duty to Queen and country. Just like at the end of Raider of the Lost Ark."

I went to view the videos.

"*Jesus!* Come here!" I shouted. It was amazing: all four cells did something different but equally inexplicable.

The 'Tom' cells broke up when played on fast-forward. When I looked back at the sample the meat was rotting despite having been frozen at minus thirty-two. For the same reason Dick should have been inactive but wasn't: the cells collided and one absorbed the other: I'd never seen anything like it! My heart was racing. Harry's were the ones that just grew smaller. Again I looked at the meta sample and found it rotting. What in hell was going on? Were they all like this, and what effect might they have on whoever ate them?

Finally Jane. Here I recognised the pattern: the cells were dying, the nucleus was becoming transparent, the whole being eaten from within.

"Bloody hell," said Oates over my shoulder. Four cells: four different behaviours. Decay, aggressive absorption, shrinkage and death. We had no idea what was going on. We sat down. QPR won three-one.

17.

I went home and drank. Oates said he wasn't feeling too clever. I'd cancelled my visit to Bristol, Lianne making it very clear she didn't want to speak to me, so it was just me and a deep-pan pepperoni. Something was niggling. Something I'd read.

Mum texted: 'You didn't call today. Me and your dad are ill, can you come over tomorrow? x' I nearly phoned but you can guess I didn't.

Watched the news: voting process announced for new Pope, Russian meteor analysed, mystery bug strikes hospital. My mind was a blur. Started watching *Match of the Day* then found myself on Googling again. Four horses, four horses...

And then... there it was in front of me: decay, aggressive absorption, shrinkage and death.

I sat for a long time. And all I could think was 'sweet Jesus, no'.

18.

I'm back! Had a drink if I'm honest. It's... what? Monday evening. I think it's because I'm nearing the end of the story. Writing has helped me go back, and taken my mind off what might be about to happen. Stories are escapism, right? Getting away from the trials and tribulations of everyday life? Getting ahead of myself, assuming you haven't already figured it out.

I slept badly. I was being chased by four horses of different colours. One red, one black, one white and the other pale green. I woke up drenched and tried to call Oates but there was no answer. Even tried calling Brinkley. I needed to do some more tests, desperately wanted to disprove something. I went in on the Sunday morning – all was quiet. Put the radio on for company.

You see when we test we test for something specific. All this time we'd been testing for horse DNA and of course we found it. Like I said, not just traces but huge chunks of it. And that didn't make sense if there were only four

111

horses. But we didn't test for other stuff like lamb or pork or dog. But I guarantee no one else was running the same test I was on that Sunday morning.

In one sense it's just another set of results. I got the target pattern off the database – default, nothing special. Radio debate was all doom and gloom – I remember wondering if Mum was listening. The hospital story had escalated – two hundred and fifty seriously ill, a few deaths – and there'd been a series of violent crimes overnight but of course the horsemeat story wouldn't go away.

Decay. Aggression. Shrinkage. Death. In my head a red light was flashing.

Went to make a drink, had to go upstairs to the machines. Got distracted by a car-crash right outside. Three cars – two blokes fighting. On a Sunday morning. Maybe one was late for church. I was past laughing then and I definitely am now. It happened so *fast.*

You can probably guess that the test was positive. In one way it proved nothing – well, it proved there was worse than horse in there, but it didn't prove what I'd come to suspect. What I feared. That Mum was right – that the silly old bat was right.

I tried to call her, suddenly wanted nothing more than to hear her voice, would have given anything to hear her ramble on about anything she wanted. Still would.

There was a funny noise from the radio – a scuffle, some shouts, then light music. I listened transfixed for ten minutes, knowing something was wrong, but it didn't stop. It's still there: I check every morning.

19.

I surfed the news channels and heard reports from all over. Once they'd linked the four tribulations – there's a world I learned – and the penny finally dropped the story grew massively: debilitating illness, death, accelerated wasting and incredible violence; the stories and pictures were horrific. I went upstairs at midday and there were police sirens and people running in the streets. I went back inside – the travel news said not to go out: the Tube had stopped, roads were barricaded. It was incredible – so fast and so utterly complete. I tried contacting Oates, then Brinkley but there was no reply. Nor from Mum, or Lianne.

I had microwave pasta that night before falling asleep on the couch watching the news roll in.

I woke on Monday confused and cold. The heating had failed, my phone battery was dead – the charger was on my desk at home – and when I tried the landlines the network was down too. Online activity had dropped: lots of '404' errors, basic format news only. Of course pretty much *everyone* must have eaten one of the four types, or eaten something else that had. I keep checking for symptoms, have done for these eight, nine weeks. So far so good.

20.

So here I am in my basement with my microscope and my laptop and I am hoping to dear God for a 'War-of-the-Worlds' type ending where the bacteria or maybe the ants or the cockroaches come to the human's aid. I can't trust anyone – there are stories of gangs luring people outside.

Waiting – that's what my life has become, if not for rescue then for death. And sometimes I wonder if sooner wouldn't be better because what comes next could be worse. You see I read up on it, on the internet. It's all there and Mum was right – she said the end had come, that the time of judgement, The Apocalypse was upon us.

113

And I saw in the right hand of him that sat on the throne a book written within and on the backside, sealed with seven seals...

And I saw when the Lamb opened one of the seals, and I heard, as it were the noise of thunder, one of the four beasts saying, Come and see.

And I saw, and behold a white horse: and he that sat on him had a bow; and a crown was given unto him: and he went forth conquering, and to conquer.

And when he had opened the second seal, I heard the second beast say, Come and see.

And there went out another horse that was red: and power was given to him that sat thereon to take peace from the earth, and that they should kill one another: and there was given unto him a great sword.

And when he had opened the third seal, I heard the third beast say, Come and see. And I beheld, and lo a black horse; and he that sat on him had a pair of balances in his hand...

And when he had opened the fourth seal, I heard the voice of the fourth beast say, Come and see.

And I looked, and behold a pale horse: and his name that sat on him was Death, and Hell followed with him. And power was given unto them over the fourth part of the earth, to kill with sword, and with hunger, and with death, and with the beasts of the earth.

Pestilence, war, famine and Death – the opening of the first four seals – four horses and four horse*men* of The Apocalypse. Harbingers of the Last Judgement – bringers of Hell on Earth. Book of Revelation – Chapter 6 verses 1-8. It's been there in black and white for the best part of two thousand years. But I think it's fair to say no one expected them to arrive in burgers.

114

So here I wait – wait for the next seal to be opened and given the sneaky way the first four arrived God knows what they'll be like. The souls of the dead rising, if I recall. Speculation is rife on the message-boards, but I wish it'd hurry up: the suspense is killing me.

21.

'No network connection' this morning. It's very quiet without the internet. You don't realise just how noisy it was. I'd give anything to be with Lianne.

About the author
Adrian Naylor took up writing ten years ago to relieve the boredom of business trips. He's written three novels and over thirty short stories he'd like to see in the horror/supernatural section of your local library. Abandoned by two grown-up children he and his wife have since been adopted by an over-eager cocker spaniel and an errant cat. They currently live in the wilds of Northumberland; the children visit.

Julia's Crackers

G. Norman Lippert

On the bus downtown, Julia Statham made a mental list of worse ways to spend a Friday night before Christmas. She was an imaginative woman. By the time she walked the last few blocks to the Warwickshire and changed out of her boots in the lobby coat-room, she'd come up with: one, being mugged; two, receiving emergency dental surgery from Gordon Ramsey; and three, having tea with her landlord.

That last was a close one. But he was an extremely creepy landlord.

She wanted to go home and hide under a blanket on the couch and binge on frozen pizza and Netflix. Instead, she followed the signs for the Taylor & Sweeney office Christmas party and pretended to be happy to see Jim Sweeney swaggering through the small crowd at her, two drinks held aloft, his unbuttoned jacket flapping.

He pressed a champagne flute into Julia's hand, watched to see if she would take a sip. Dutifully, she did.

"I've got a special gift just for you," he said, and plucked a cracker from his pocket.

"How thoughtful." It was wrapped in gold paper with tartan ribbons.

"Oh, not that," he laughed, then leaned close to her cheek, bringing along the overpowering odour of wine breath and Brylcreem. "It's in the Secret Santa gifts," he whispered against her ear. She tried not to recoil. "On the table by the punch. I hope you like it as much as I do."

He gave her a conspiratorial wink, as subtle as a Whoopie cushion at a funeral.

"Oh! Bloody hell," Julia tipped the champagne onto her

sleeve. "I'm so clumsy. Excuse me, Mr. Sweeney." She made a show of awkward shrugs, blushing, backing away, and nearly fled to the washroom; which wasn't easy.

She eventually found it in the hall, across from the elevators.

It was brightly lit and immaculate, merciless with white tiles and wall length mirrors. She dabbed her sleeve with damp towels, looked at herself in the mirror, and blew a disgruntled breath into her mousy brown bangs.

Another woman was in the washroom with her. Julia only noticed her when she approached the same row of sinks to check her perfect hair, touch up her flawless, if subtle make-up.

"Sweeney is like everybody else at this party," the woman commented to her reflection, leaning to examine her lipstick. "They all see themselves through the wrong end of the telescope."

Julia blinked aside at the woman. She was almost disconcertingly perfect. Julia's age, but utterly composed, exuding confidence.

Timidly, Julia ventured, "What do you mean?"

The woman gave a businesslike sigh. "The wrong end of the telescope. Sweeney *thinks* he's a giant. A captain of industry, top of the heap, every woman's lip-biting fantasy, albeit for his fat wallet more than his fat arse."

Julia choked a little laugh. "Do I know you?"

"You're not the only office girl getting a 'special gift' from him on the Secret Santa table. I imagine that doesn't shock you much." The woman looked aside at Julia, turned to face her. Julia faltered a bit beneath her gaze. The woman was everything Julia had ever dreamed of being.

"I... Did he give one to you, too?"

The woman smiled wryly and shifted her gaze away. "If he did it would be a fatal mistake. The point is, he's got loads of lines in the water. You don't have to be the fish that bites. Only weak fishies bite."

Julia considered this. She frowned a little.

The woman stepped closer, coming next to Julia, facing her. In a lower voice, accompanied by a sly smile, she said, "Don't worry. I took care of it."

Her tone of voice made Julia's shoulders tense. "What do you mean?"

Across from her, the woman's smile turned sly. She gave a half shrug. "I put his wife's name on all of his 'special gifts'. She's about to open half a dozen sweet little nothings, none of which could possibly fit her fairly generous shape."

Julia took a moment to absorb this idea. Her eyes widened, both in amazement and a little trepidation. "Will he know it was you?"

The woman brushed it off, turning away again. "Who cares? It could've been any of the women in the office he's been stringing along. But oh! What I'd give to be a fly on the wall of their house tonight. My, yes."

Julia watched the woman, awed. She realized that she was staring and turned away quickly. She balled up the damp towels and threw them away. She looked in her purse for her own lipstick and pulled out the cracker that Sweeney had given her.

The woman leaned closer, looked down at the cracker in Julia's hand.

"Let's do it, you and I. Right now."

Julia blinked up at the woman in surprise, then laughed a little, embarrassed, her cheeks reddening.

She held out the cracker. The woman took the other end in her perfectly manicured, strong hand.

They pulled.

The crack echoed from the tiles. A small white box fell

to the counter, and the woman reached to collect it.

"Personalized golf ball markers," she sighed, straightening and showing the box to Julia. "How perfectly typical." She offered the box to Julia. The Taylor & Sweeney logo was printed on it blue letters.

Julia shook her head. "I don't golf."

The woman's smile resurfaced. Her eyes glittered. "I know."

Julia went back to the party feeling confused, but a bit more cheerful. She watched the Secret Santa table. Later, she danced with another young intern called Molly.

"The pig," Molly breathed, watching Sweeney by the bar. "He's been pressuring me to go on a 'business trip' with him."

"To Bruges," Julia nodded.

Molly glared at her, and then broke into a grin. "Are you quite serious?"

In a mock man's voice, Julia said, "It could do wonders for your legal career, my pet."

Molly brayed laughter and threw an arm around Julia.

Later, they watched a puzzled-looking Missus Sweeney carry an armload of small, identical gifts to the elevator.

As far as Julia recalled, the woman from the washroom never showed up at the party. In fact, Julia didn't see her again until almost exactly a year later.

Snow was falling beyond the plate windows of the tenth floor offices of Taylor & Muldoon as Julia waited for the elevator. She bobbed impatiently on her toes, her purse clutched in both fists like a stress toy. She stabbed at the DOWN button again, and glanced behind her.

The bell dinged and the steel doors shuttled open, revealing a thankfully empty interior. She hurried inside, punched the button for the lobby, and turned around. The hall leading back toward the office was empty.

119

She closed her eyes and shook her head, making her hair flop against her cheeks.

"Stupid, stupid, *stupid!*" she rasped to herself as the doors slid shut.

She opened her eyes again, and wished she hadn't. Reflected in the steel elevator doors she saw herself as he would have. She looked like a prim, bleached mummy dressed in a frumpy, too conservative pantsuit. She teased her limp hair, then gave up. It would do no good. The damage was done.

The elevator slowed, shimmied to a stop. Too soon for the lobby. Julia backed up a step and fixed her gaze on the illuminated floor numbers.

The doors opened and someone stepped in. A woman. Julia didn't look at her.

The doors closed.

The elevator began to descend again.

"He's more nervous than you are, you know."

Julia blinked rapidly and frowned. She looked at the woman next to her.

She was in a chocolate brown pantsuit this time. On her it looked halfway between the boardroom and the bedroom. Her dark hair shone in the light like ebony.

"You again," Julia said, before she could stop herself.

The woman gave a light, self-deprecating gesture with her hands and nodded. Then she said, "He barely heard a word that came out of your mouth."

Julia shook her head in consternation. "Excuse me, but do I actually know you? Do you work here?"

"Yes and yes," she answered, half smiling, watching Julia with disconcerting familiarity. "But that's not what you really want to ask, I think."

Julia was in no mood. She turned ahead, glared at the elevator doors. "Do tell. What do I really want to ask?"

"What's in the note I sent him in your name."

Julia jolted and nearly dropped her purse. She wheeled on the woman incredulously. "Why would you...!?" She collected herself. "You didn't. You don't even know what you're talking about."

"Hey, Daniel," the woman recited, tilting her head and raising her eyes. "You said you had never even seen snow until you were nineteen. Ever made a snowball? Come to the rooftop terrace at six forty-five and see if you can throw like a girl."

Julia's mouth fell open in utter horror. She snapped it shut and shook her head fervently. "You didn't."

"Love, 'Juliet'."

"Juliet!?"

"That's what he called you during his first week on the job, isn't it?"

Julia was nearly apoplectic. "Yes! Because he couldn't be bothered to remember my actual name!"

"Oh, I forgot," the woman rolled her eyes and smirked, "you don't remember much Shakespeare, do you?"

The elevator slowed and stopped. As soon as the doors parted, Julia squeezed through. Her heels clacked on the marble floor as she hurried to the revolving lobby doors.

Behind her, the woman called, "He said, 'enjoy your family holiday in Skegness', and you said 'thanks, you too'."

Julia skidded and stopped. She didn't look back at the woman. She boiled for a moment in a stew of high anxiety. Then, jerkily, she half-turned.

"Are you supposed to be my fairy godmother or something?" There was a plaintive, desperate note in her voice. "Because my *actual* godmother is very much alive in Oxbridge."

The woman stood in the open doors of the elevator,

121

looking as infuriatingly cool and fresh as a spring bloom. Her voice was gentle now, but firm. "I just know how much this means to you, despite what you keep telling yourself. But you'll need this."

She produced something from her own small, natty purse.

Julia deflated. "A cracker."

The woman's smile was warm now. "It's kind of our thing, I've decided." She held it out.

Julia glared at her, torn, breathing hard through her nose. Then, as if hating herself for it, she stalked back to the elevator.

"You make me *feel* crackers," she growled under her breath, taking the other end.

They pulled. With a pop, an object fell into Julia's hand. It was a cheap silver ring.

"Lose it when you're playing on the roof terrace," the woman smiled secretively. "Then let him find it for you."

"That's ridiculous."

The woman shrugged. "Clock's ticking." She tapped her wrist and stepped backwards into the waiting elevator. It dinged and the elevator doors eased shut before her, as if on cue.

Julia stood impaled on indecision, her half of the cracker and the cheap silver ring in her hands. Then, almost in a panic, she stabbed at the UP button repeatedly.

The clock in the lobby informed her that it was already ten to seven.

When she arrived at the rooftop terrace, Daniel was waiting for her, huddled against the cold and the falling snow, but smiling uncertainly.

The snow was too cold to pack. They ended up snogging a little instead.

Over the following weeks Julia wondered about the

mysterious woman. Dimly, she questioned her own sanity. She'd been under a lot of stress, after all. And yet as she and Daniel began the heady whirlwind of dating, and Julia's own legal career began to shift into higher gear, gaining her increasing opportunities and attention, she soon forgot the infuriatingly suave, cool, gorgeous woman – her capricious benefactor.

Until the following December, one week before Christmas.

She was on the bus, glaring blindly into the blurred tableaux of the city, her mind whirring, full of nearly debilitating worries, stress, and dark omens.

"You should do some power poses," the passenger next to her suggested helpfully.

Julia startled in her seat. She recognized the voice, of course. "You again!?"

"That's what you said last time. You're going to have to get used to me eventually." The woman sat primly, perfectly at ease, next to Julia.

Julia fumed. "I don't have time for this! What do you want?"

"I want you to do some power poses," she repeated. She straightened in her seat, thrust out her chest, and lifted her sculpted chin. "I am indomitable! I am unstoppable! I am a force of nature! Come on, say it with me."

Julia stared at her, open-mouthed. "You're making fun of me!"

The woman relaxed and sighed affectionately. "None of the sort. But you do take yourself a bit too seriously. Admittedly, it's what's driven you this far. But now it's time to relax a bit and let your guard down."

Julia slumped and hugged her purse. "There couldn't be any *worse* time for that advice."

"Mr. Taylor wouldn't be interviewing you for junior

123

partner if he hadn't already decided you deserve it."

Julia shot another shocked glance at the woman. "Nobody knows about that except me and the partners!"

"Just like nobody knows that Daniel's been hinting at proposing to you for the past month and you're scared witless about it because you think he's too starry-eyed to see what a mess you are."

"You really have to stop doing this," Julia breathed shrilly, collapsing against the seat and taking her face in her hands. "You're driving me mad. I don't know how you know all this. I don't even know who you are."

The woman lowered her velvety voice and cocked her head. "Don't tell me you really haven't figured it out by now."

Julia shook her head and laughed weakly. "I'm sure I don't know *what* you're talking about."

"Do you remember the first thing I ever said to you?"

Julia was still shaking her head. "You showed up in the washroom and said you'd taken care of randy old Sweeney."

"No. I said that everyone at the party sees themselves through the wrong end of the telescope. Sweeney thought he was a big, powerful icon, but he was really just an insecure little pillock hiding behind an inflated ego. You, on the other hand… well, you're rather the opposite."

Julia blew a weary sigh and glared out the window. "You sound like my mum."

"That shouldn't come as much of a surprise, really."

Julia turned and glared at the woman again. Her smile was knowing, her head tilted provocatively, one eyebrow raised.

After a pause, breathlessly, Julia whispered, "Oh… my God."

"You're seeing it now, aren't you?"

Julia's mind whirled back to the first time she'd met the mysterious, amazing, dismaying, remarkable woman. In the washroom, by the mirror.

The second time: standing before the steel elevator doors.

And now, in the bus, next to the window...

I've been looking at my reflection the whole time.

The woman mirrored in the bus window nodded. The smile on her face was smug but warm. "You didn't recognize me because you couldn't see yourself the way everyone else does. It's time for that to change."

Julia's head swam. She fell back against the seat again. She closed her eyes.

The woman's voice was her own. It spoke in her thoughts now, soft but teasingly emboldened. *Seeing yourself as everyone else does is only the first step. Accepting Daniel's love, and Mr. Taylor's trust, is only the beginning. It's time to show them, and everyone else, that you've only just begun.*

She opened her eyes again and looked aside into the window glass.

The woman was still there, as beautiful and confident and audaciously vibrant as ever. She smiled at Julia as Julia smiled at her. Because she *was* Julia. She had been the whole time.

The bus droned on.

Five minutes later, one block from the offices of the soon to be Taylor, Muldoon, & Statham, the bus stopped. The woman got off.

She stopped and looked at herself in the window of Fortnum & Mason's. She nodded with satisfaction.

As she walked, snow began to fall.

Relaxed and confident, she nailed the interview.

Afterward, she found a cracker sitting on her desk. She

picked it up, examined it, smiled a little slyly.

It's kind of my thing, she thought, and set it carefully on the corner of her desk, leaving it as a symbol: mysterious, but bursting with potential.

Just like Julia herself.

About the author

G. Norman Lippert's first published short story was published by Hugo and Nebula award winning author Orson Scott Card (*The Long Way Home, Intergalactic Medicine Show*, 2011).

Since then, his body of more than a dozen books and stories have accumulated nearly 40,000 reviews on goodreads.com, with an average four-star rating.

He currently lives in Erie, Pennsylvania with his wife and two children.

Rescue Me, Saving You

Linda Flynn

John Staines celebrated the first day of his retirement by buying his wife a shiny red Mazda. Then he stood back in his front garden as she drove off, out of his life in it, the metallic gleam disappearing into the sunset.

It didn't take long for John to learn that when Priscilla folded herself and her blonde bob into the driving seat, they hadn't gone far. She parked at Barney the plumber's at number 46; an acquaintance that had developed when their pipes had needed lagging.

All that was left of John's retirement bonus was the elaborate gilt and rather distasteful carriage clock that had been presented. It seemed he was given it to watch its interminable ticking, now that his life no longer needed to revolve around clocks. Time hung heavily.

The company retained Priscilla's services, but no longer had any need for his "pernickety perfectionism." Technology could deal with the more fastidious details. In any case, they could employ two younger people for his salary, a two for one deal.

John discovered that if he leaned out of his bathroom window, he could see number 46 quite clearly. He started to jog along the road and into the park, as though his speed would make the day move faster. Each time he would look in through their windows, memorising all the details.

One morning he slid along the park track with his head lowered, when he had a sensation of being followed. His hood was wrapped around his head and rain ran in rivulets down his face. Mud slithered over his legs as his trainers slipped and squelched. There was a sniffing, snuffling, panting sound around his heels.

John looked down at a creature with mud mangled fur. He kept running. So did the dog, keeping perfect time. Never before had John been the recipient of so much attention.

At the end of the park the dog looked up expectantly. He was bedraggled, without a lead or collar, so John wound his scarf around the dog's neck and marched him to the vet's. No identichip was found and no reports of a missing border collie. It seemed as though they had found each other.

When the vet asked if she could record a name for the dog, he looked at its downcast tail, shrugged a sagging shoulder and said, "Droopy."

As John ran a bath for Droopy, he recalled how his wife hated any kind of a mess. He rummaged under the sink for his wife's favourite organic shampoo and rubbed a little into his fur. Droopy shook it out. Soon the entire bathroom, from the fitted ceiling lights to the white tiles was flicked with mud splats.

In the airing cupboard he pulled out the fluffiest Egyptian cotton towels to rub Droopy down.

Meal time was a little more problematic. Although he had bought some dog food from the vet's, he'd forgotten the bowls. Scouring the cupboards he found his wife's two favourite ceramic dishes which were an ideal size for a water bowl and Chunky Paws dog food.

John removed the lid off Priscilla's large sewing basket and laid it on the floor. He rolled up several of her softest cashmere jumpers – "cashmore" he used to call them as they had cost her a fortune. These could be the ballast at the bottom of the dog bed. He found a particularly downy alpaca scarf, which he laid over the top.

Droopy appreciated all of these preparations for his day bed, but at night time he padded after John up the stairs and slept on his wife's side of bed.

Unable to sleep, John crept down the road. The metallic car winked provocatively in the street light. He waited until midnight when they switched off and then he attached some empty cans with string to the underside of the car. He wrote Just Married in Priscilla's favourite lipstick across the rear windscreen and as an extra, stuck the contents from one of the tins of sardines into the radiator grill. John knew that when she left the house at exactly 7.15 in the morning, that she would disturb all of the neighbours.

When he returned to snuggle up to Droopy, he slept surprisingly soundly, with just the dog's snoring reverberating around the room.

At first the two of them just mooched around together, until a neighbour's cat leapt into a tree next door. Droopy cleared the fence in seconds, and the next one and the rest of the row. Breathless, John caught up with him at the end of the road, but it gave him an idea.

He started to assemble an assortment of obstacles in his back garden, beginning with mini jumps. Droopy was fast and surprisingly agile. Next he added in a tunnel and coaxed him through it, followed by a hoop to jump through. Finally a row of bamboo canes made the weave, which droopy learned to wind his body around at speed.

Every morning they eagerly practised, becoming faster and faster. But still he watched number 46 when he had time, assisted now by some binoculars he had bought.

On another sleepless night John crept into Barney's front garden, armed with a spray containing bleach and weed killer. For twenty minutes he sprayed the letters BASTARD across the lawn, adding a few extra flourishes. John had always been good at art at school and found the process immensely satisfying.

Droopy's training continued apace, particularly when they joined a couple of agility clubs. They learned how to use the A frame, dog walk and see-saw. As he fine-tuned their technique, he also taught Droopy to sit stay. The collie was quick and clever, the perfect pupil.

A few weeks passed in no time and they registered to take part in some trials, with a view to participating in competitions. John improved his own fitness, but also learned how to direct his own body language, as his dog responded to the slightest gesture.

Every day they shortened their timing and sharpened their precision. So great was their absorption that they didn't hear a scribbled note being thrust through their letter box from Priscilla, requesting the return of her clothes.

John approached the task with his customary precision. He neatly folded the remaining items in Priscilla's wardrobe, carefully layering them with tissue paper. He added a few items of his own. These were placed in large boxes, all of which were labelled with her name in large bold lettering.

He unloaded the boxes into the office block around lunch time. Tony the doorman gave John a cursory nod, whilst Paula on reception smiled and buzzed Priscilla when he showed her the note.

He piled the boxes on top of each other, ensuring that P. Staines was clearly displayed. Just before he departed, he quickly reached inside and activated the sex toys hidden in the bottom boxes. He hastily slipped through the doors as the buzzing and vibrating began.

A moment later security was called, but John only threw a backward glance at the confusion. He was dimly aware of some sirens flashing in the distance.

Already John's mind was thinking about the qualifying Agility Competition, the one which could take them all the way to Crufts.

The pair moved like a single unit, with Droopy obeying

every gesture, every command to twist, turn, jump. The angles were sharp, defined, precise. John's heart hammered at the speed, pushing them on further, faster, better.

He didn't see Priscilla amongst the spectators, bobbing around in her seat with excitement, not even when she gave a little wave or stood up to cheer amidst the roaring crowd when they won their round. It was just him and Droopy dog a.k.a. Mr Mud Mangler Give Em Welly.

About the author
Linda Flynn has had two children's and one book for teenagers published. In addition she has had twelve short stories (for adults, children and young adults) as well as a number of newspaper and magazine articles printed. Her first writing commission was for six educational books with the Heinemann Fiction Project. Linda is also a writer for the Medical Detection Dogs charity.

Sheep Be Damned

Dianne Stadhams

"To be or not to be the Fifth Sheep?" I repeat aloud in panic.

My part is twenty lines in total. One line is repeated. As Fifth Sheep I get to say, "Oh no it's a dwarf singing hi ho" once in act one, twice in act two. The remaining seventeen lines offer the same depth of characterisation and scope for interpretation and delivery.

I'm told by the Director that the Fifth Sheep is essential to the success of this show.

Pull the other one, I want to say. It's the village pantomime. The audience is one hundred adults and pumpkin-faced kids in nappies.

The Fifth Sheep has three more lines than the Sixth Sheep and three less than the Fourth. The script writer, another villager, enjoys a reputation for numeracy, fairness and accuracy. I've been doubly promoted this year – jumped from Seventh Sheep of last year. Sheep feature in every show whatever the theme. *Snow White*, *Jack and the Beanstalk*, *Cinderella...* ten sheep wow the crowd annually.

The Tenth Sheep has a mere five lines and is struggling with those. Not the words themselves, just the order of delivery. But the cast and village understand. It's wonderful that Maureen, she of tenth sheep fame, can still tread the boards with Alzheimer's.

Tonight is the dress rehearsal. I am not a happy mutton chop. My costume is a disaster.

"You can't be serious,' I complain, yet again, "I'll be a laughing stock in this."

I say this loudly to anyone in the communal dressing room who will listen. Nobody does listen. I can see that the cast are too busy preening their own costumes, lovingly stitched from abandoned curtains and old pillow cases, by Mrs Jackson and her fleet of biddies. The loyal seamstresses are from the retirement village. They chew on their false teeth as they sew a last minute, distressed hem or two.

My costume is a sack made from something synthetic like they use for stuffing sofas. It may be fire retardant and work wonders for health and safety but it does little for a thirty something, avocado shaped, virgin-in-hope.

"How men see me," I groan.

I know the costume was originally made to fit a morbidly obese eleven year old in the school's nativity play. There is plenty of width so I try to pleat it. The tucks merely emphasise my ample waist. The real structural challenge lies in the length. The original model was ten centimetres shorter than me. The scratchy material and the ever rising crutch of the costume threaten the circulation to my private parts. Mrs Jackson tries to be kind and tells me I look quite enticing.

She lies.

"God please let me get promoted to Third Sheep next year," I pray silently. I recall that particular costume was originally constructed for the tallest boy in the primary school.

"Better still persuade the Director to make me second tree. Then I get to swank on stage in a silky green satin sheath."

I really, really want to wake up Frank, the short-sighted fellow on the lighting rig, to show him what he might enjoy. He hasn't noticed me yet. He hangs round with the fellows on the set and avoids the women… of any age. He even blushes when Mrs Jackson says hello.

I left an old copy of the local paper near where Frank likes to sit. The front page has a picture of me winning a major prize at the summer fete. It's quite flattering I think although you can't really see much of my face because my hat has slipped forward. Just as well because it was really hot that day and my face was more beetroot than pale and interesting.

I grow castor oil plants for homeopathic purposes and marrows. Jealous detractors whisper that their size cannot be natural. Last year I had a burglary. The door to my garden shed was forced. I told the police that nothing appeared to have been stolen. Mrs Jackson reckoned that the unwelcome visitor was a spy sent to identify steroids that enhanced marrow growth. Bets have been placed on who did what and when. I think it was the Stage Manager who is a recognised expert on all things scientific in the village. The police didn't arrest anyone. No evidence they said, so I bought a padlock this year just to be sure.

With any marrows that don't win ribbons I make jam for the cast in our annual panto.

"No surprises with the jam this year?" a cast member enquires. "I thought you might have followed my advice and added some ginger."

It's difficult not to attract the odd bitchy comment when you're a winner. I rise above it and don't reply. The offending cast member still takes a jar I notice.

Most of the cast avoid me along with the rest of the sheep. Our costumes stink from years of sweating under the lights. The fabric doesn't breathe. It can't be washed. There is no budget for dry cleaning. No one is permitted to take their costume home from the village hall, ever, for any reason. Orders come from the Director and Stage Manager about this every year. To disobey means demotion or even exclusion from next year's production. Conformity gives us strength in numbers. So, dressed as a sheep, I am resigned to act as a sheep and bleat no more.

My life may seem drab to most of the cast. But I have a secret pleasure which I share with no one from the village. They wouldn't understand.

By sheer chance I discovered an Internet group dedicated to the virtual re-enactment of *Gone with the Wind*. To the on-line membership I am a goddess, the living embodiment of everything Scarlett O'Hara was and ever could be. I am word perfect with the entire film script. My southern American drawl is enticingly authentic. Scarlett's wardrobe moulds perfectly to my avatar body. I have numerous Rhett Butlers duelling over me to attract my favour. In cyberspace they can see only my perfection. I am Scarlett, number 1091.

Tonight I am a terrified thespian, not a fearless Scarlett. The final straw is this costume. I burst into tears. Those in the dressing room slide away. It is not considered good form to be emotional back stage.

Mrs Jackson takes me aside and asks, "What's wrong, pet? You'll be fine. And the costume is okay. Especially when all of you sheep are on stage. Looks kind of cute actually."

"You don't understand," I say and start blubbering again.

"Try me."

"I've told a lie," I whisper.

"We all tell lies," Mrs Jackson cajoles.

"Not like this one," I reply, "it's a whopper. Like ten hail Mary's worth."

Mrs Jackson goes to the corner of the room and pours me a tepid cup of herbal tea from the large enamel pot. The spout is wonky and liquid dribbles down the side and onto the table where the wigs for the seven dwarves are slung in a pile. Hygiene is not an issue for the cast. I think it should be after I heard the primary school has had an infestation of

135

nits. She gives me the tea, smiles sweetly and whispers into my ear, "Didn't Scarlett tell a few to make life work?"

"You know?" I gasp.

"Your secret's safe with me."

"How did you find out?" I ask her.

"First principle of gossip: never reveal your sources. Nobody here knows about your Scarlett or follows the blog. I promise I won't say anything."

"Yes but Rhett might!"

"Sorry pet, you've lost me," she says handing me a tissue. Sheep make-up is running down my cheeks. I'm morphing into a zebra.

"Rhett Butler, number 532, from Reading, is coming. He has emailed me. He says nothing can deter him from attending my play. He's pledged to travel to wherever I'm performing," I explain.

"Well that's wonderful isn't it? He'll get to see you can play lots of different roles. Versatile can be very sexy."

"Somehow he thinks I'm the leading lady," I sob.

"Well you can clear that up when you meet. Honestly that costume is alright. It certainly shows off your legs. And cream is a good colour on stage under the lights."

"He thinks it's a professional production."

"He'll work out that it's not. But don't worry. You're good, really good. I'm sure a fifth sheep on the London stage wouldn't do the role any better than you."

"The Seduction of Snow White by the Dalek Dwarves," I wail.

"What?"

"I might have said that the name of the show was…"

"He's in for a bit of a surprise then. It's a bit more wholesome than he is probably expecting."

"A snuff script on stage," I cry. "That's what he circulated to the group."

Mrs Jackson can't think of an honest reply.

"What else did he email you to say?" she asks.

"Show me your apples and I'll show you my banana."

"Mmm, I can see your problem," says Mrs Jackson as she exits the dressing room to check backstage.

I am bereft. My unmasking is imminent. There can be a no more dramatic denouement. I know that if I tell the truth my life on earth will be ruined in addition to any potential in cyberspace. The trolls will bury me. My reputation is trashed. There will be no credits to roll if I am named and shamed to my band of Margaret Mitchell groupies. No more will I be Scarlett the harlot hashtag. No more will I be adored by Rhett Butlers around the world.

Nobody will give a damn.

Not even Frank from lighting!

About the author

Dianne Stadhams is an Australian, resident in the UK, who works globally in poverty alleviation, peace and reconciliation projects and has a PhD in communications for development. Her website www.stadhams.com gives details. She has two plays in development with Bristol Old Vic, a collection of illustrated short stories accepted for publication, and two novels in final edit, one of which was shortlisted for a global competition.

Snap

Karen Kendrick

It would be the kind of party I would never throw and was seldom invited to. I looked at the personalised invitation, tasteful and expensive looking; posh, Mum would have said. I dropped it into the paper bin and went to make a cup of tea.

While it was brewing I opened my laptop, intending to work. The page gleamed at me like a Hollywood smile; come on, write on me then. The words started to form but when I put them on the pearly whiteness they seemed wrong, jumbled. I hit delete.

The phone rang out shrilly and I almost dropped the computer. I placed it down and went over to the phone.

"Hello?"

"God, Mum, you always sound so worried. It's only me."

"Helen. What's wrong?"

"There's nothing wrong. It's Boxing Day. I was wondering if we could visit."

"Oh. Erm… well, actually I'm on my way out."

"Really?" Her voice was full of scepticism.

"Yes, actually. I've been invited to George and Sheila's party, and I've decided to go."

"You're going to a party?"

"Yes, I thought I would."

"It's a fancy dress party. Did you know that?"

I paused, wondering how far I could really stretch this lie. Oh, what the hell. "Yes, I know. I have a costume already."

I could hear Helen's voice saying to somebody "She's going to a fancy dress party!" I heard Mark's soft laughter.

"Find out what she's going as."

"You're not on mute, you know," I said, evilly.

"Well, what *are* you going as? You can't blame us for laughing. It's pretty hilarious, Mum."

I thought for a moment, and glanced at the remnants of my lunch on the plate.

"A cracker!"

More laughter at the other end.

"A cracker. You're going as a Christmas cracker."

"Yes. I've had the costume for years."

This bit was true, actually. I really did have a cracker costume stowed away in the loft, unworn since 1976.

The line went silent. This time Helen had remembered the mute button. A moment or two later she was back.

"You know, Mum, we had an invitation too. We weren't going to bother, but Mark thinks it would be fun, and we could see you at the same time."

Amusement laced her every syllable.

"Oh. Are you sure? I don't think it's your usual sort of thing."

"Mum, with respect, how could you possibly know what my sort of thing is? I'm not sixteen anymore."

"No," I sighed. "No, I suppose you're not."

"So, how are you getting there? Would you like a lift?"

"Alright," I hear myself saying.

"Great. We'll be there at four. Looking forward to seeing the costume!"

I heard the line go dead. I placed the receiver up to my burning face. What had just happened?

I searched my brain for a plausible excuse. I waited for an hour, and then rang her back to tell her of my sudden crippling migraine. The phone rang and rang and eventually went to her voicemail. I lost courage at the last minute and hung up.

Damn. I really was going to have to go. And dressed as a Christmas cracker.

I climbed up into the loft and began opening unmarked boxes filled with memories. Photo albums, from the days before social media. I opened one at random and looked at a picture from my university days. A snapshot from a drunken night out, slightly blurred. I stopped the wave of nostalgia in its tracks, snorting at my silliness. Those days were no better, really. I was just young enough for it not to matter so much.

The costume was at the bottom of a box of clothes I had never expected to wear again but couldn't quite part with. I pulled it out, feeling nauseous. Was it always that short or had it somehow shrunk while in storage? I imagined myself walking into the party, twig-like old woman legs and shrunken cleavage displayed for all to see, like some sort of grotesque aging ex-film star. I buried my head in my hands.

Helen arrived at 4 p.m. precisely. Mark was a stickler for punctuality, a trait left over from his army days.

I had compromised by wearing the tiny dress over a pair of smart flared trousers and wrapping a silver scarf around my shoulders. I still felt ridiculous, especially when I put the hat on.

"Mum! You look great!"

Helen was dressed in an elf costume, which I thought an odd choice for a forty year old woman.

"I do not. I look, and feel, stupid."

"No, honestly. It's a nice costume. Where did you get it?"

"I've had it for years. The last time I wore it I was a young woman."

"Well, come on. Mark and the kids are waiting."

I hobbled over to the car, realising why I so rarely wore shoes with a heel. Helen held the rear door open for me.

Two small faces looked out at me.

"Grandma, you look beautiful!" This was Summer, the youngest of the two.

"Thank you. So do you," I replied. She was dressed in an arrangement of taffeta and silk.

"I'm a Christmas fairy," she said.

Her brother stared at me silently. "Hello, Cameron," I said. He didn't reply.

"Cam, don't be rude," snapped Helen. "He's just a bit wary of people he doesn't see very often."

This was a barb in my direction, which I chose to ignore.

A short drive brought us to George and Sheila's grand house. They'd had it built a few years ago and loved to throw parties in which they could show off their large kitchen complete with island (made from recommissioned timber, of course, blah blah *blah*). I would never have come here under normal circumstances.

"Cheer up, Mum. You might enjoy yourself."

"I doubt that."

We parked on the street and walked the length of the impressive driveway, which had been lit with soft yellow lights. The door was open; there were already quite a lot of people here.

I saw her almost immediately. My instinct was to turn and flee, no matter how cold it was outside, no matter how difficult it would be to get home.

"Mother, whatever's wrong now?" asked Helen.

"I can't go in there," I say, backing up towards the door and bumping into another guest.

"Why on earth not?" She turned around to see where I was looking. "Oh, Mum. Don't be silly. Yours is much better, anyway."

At first I didn't understand what she meant. "Oh. Oh!

141

You think I'm upset because she's dressed as a cracker."

Helen frowned. "Well, what is it then?"

How could I explain this to her? I just shook my head.

"Well, you're going to have to get over it. We're not leaving. Come on, take your coat off and we'll get a drink."

I followed her in, trying to avoid making eye contact with any of the guests.

"Jane! I don't believe it! How did you work this miracle, Helen?"

"Oh, hello George. Yes, thank you for the invitation." I hoped I didn't sound as awkward as I felt.

"Come on. Get a drink. Let me take your coats. Sheila's around somewhere, but you know what she's like, probably three sheets to the wind by now. Make yourselves at home."

I was handed a glass of something sparkling with pomegranate seeds at the bottom. I held it in front of me like a shield against social contact.

"Mum, I'm going to mingle," sighed Helen. "Try to do the same. I'll be back soon."

I stood next to the oversized Christmas tree in the lounge feeling like a tremendous fool. I thought I was alone in the room until I heard a loud sigh. I looked around the tree and saw Cameron sitting on the floor behind what looked like fake presents.

"Oh. Hello," I said.

"Hello Grandma," he replied, without enthusiasm.

"Don't you want to be here either?" I asked. He shook his head.

"Mum said we only have to be here a couple of hours. But I reckon we'll be here all night."

"God, I hope not."

"Me too."

I stared at my grandson. "Why aren't you wearing a costume?"

"I just refused."

"Wish I'd thought of that."

A loud laugh sounded in the next room. Without thinking, I moved further behind the tree.

"Grandma, are you trying to avoid someone?" asked Cameron.

I nodded. "Everyone."

"Mum says you're a miscreant."

I smiled. "I think you mean a misanthrope."

"What does that mean?"

"It means I don't like people very much. I suppose she's right, I am."

"Do you like me?"

I smiled at my grandson. "Yes, you're one of the few people I do like."

A moment or two later Helen appeared. "Mum, have you seen Cam anywhere? All the other kids are in the conservatory."

"No, sorry," I lied. "But I'm sure he hasn't gone far."

"Why don't you come in the other room? You're missing the party."

"I know. That's the idea."

"Come on, Mum. Let's get you another drink."

She took my arm and steered me into the kitchen. The other Christmas cracker was standing next to the island, staring at me, looking anything but pleased.

She had always been beautiful, even back when we were university pals. She was far taller than me and effortlessly elegant. Her Christmas cracker outfit looked like it could be Dior, unlike my charity shop chic ensemble.

"Jane," she said, coldly.

"So you two know each other?" asked Helen, oblivious to the drop in temperature.

"We went to university together," I blustered. "Hello Annette. How are you?"

"Oh, you know. Well, please excuse me."

She picked up her glass and left the kitchen. Helen stared at me.

"What was that about?"

I avoided looking at her. "Oh, I think we fell out back then. I can't really remember."

"Mum. Come on."

I shrugged. "Perhaps we should leave," I said, pleadingly.

Helen glared at me. "Do you know how many parties we get to these days? I'm going nowhere unless you explain what's going on."

I didn't speak so she huffed off. The other women in the kitchen were determinedly looking away. I found another glass of wine and was about to leave when suddenly the kitchen seemed to become full of people.

"This way, everyone, I want to raise a toast."

George was herding everyone in. I couldn't sneak out, either; he was standing at the door like a bulldog.

When the last of the guests had entered the kitchen George tapped his glass and the chatter gradually diminished. George cleared his throat to prepare for one of his long, painfully dull speeches, but before he could begin his wife Sheila crashed into the room.

"Oh, have you finished already, darling?" she asked, unsteadily.

"No, I'm just…"

"Oh, my goodness, look! What a pair of crackers!" To my horror she took my sleeve and Annette's and pulled us into the middle of the room. "Snap!" She began to laugh. Some of the guests joined in nervously.

Annette gave her a withering look.

George was becoming impatient. "Come on now, Sheila, I'm waiting to…"

"Just a moment. I need to take a picture. You two stand next to each other. Could you put your arms around each other? What? What's wrong? Annette?"

"Enough is enough." She disentangled herself from Sheila and left the kitchen.

"Well! Rude!" exclaimed Sheila.

Everybody turned to look at me. I couldn't stand it.

"Excuse me," I said, and left too.

I went back to the sitting room, which was still empty. I sat on the edge of the sofa, kneading my hands nervously.

"Grandma? Is that you?"

"Hi Cam. You're still in here then."

"Yes. I've got my phone with me so I'm watching YouTube. Do you want to join me?"

I actually considered his offer. "No, thank you," I said, eventually. "I'd stick out like a sore thumb and then we'd both be caught. I'll just wait here for your mother to come and drag me off again."

"OK."

We sank back into conspiratorial silence. A few minutes later Helen did appear, looking cross.

"What an earth was all that about, Mum? What's going on with you two?"

"Oh, just old woman stuff. An argument from years ago."

"About what?"

"It was an academic argument that got out of control. Not that it's any of your business."

Helen frowned at me. "It seemed like more than that, Mum. What's really going on?"

I just shrugged and avoided her eyes.

"Is her husband here?" asked Helen.

145

"Why?" I asked, a little too sharply.

"She's upset. I thought I should let him know."

"No!" Helen gave me a surprised look. "No, I think you should let someone else do that. In fact, we really should leave."

She rolled her eyes. "Over an academic argument from 20 years ago?"

I nodded.

She looked at me sharply. "Hang on – was that why you resigned?"

"Yes. It became rather nasty."

"I always wondered. It seemed such an odd thing to do." She had a thoughtful look in her eyes which was making me nervous. "Come on," she said, turning towards the door.

"What?" I asked, warily.

"We're going to sort it out. It's ridiculous, two grown women behaving like this after twenty years."

"No, Helen, you don't understand. You don't know the full story."

"Then tell me," she said, stopping. I stared at her open mouthed.

"Well, I'm going to find Annette. Perhaps she'll tell me what's going on."

I scuttled after her as quickly as I could in my stupid shoes, protesting loudly. Helen marched on ahead of me, a blonde juggernaut crashing through the carefully constructed lies of twenty years.

"Really, Helen, you have no idea what you're doing. If we can leave I'll tell you the truth."

"No, you won't. You'll retreat even further into your woman-cave and we'll never see you again. I want to know what happened twenty years ago to turn you into – you."

I stared at my daughter, feeling the last of my resolve snap away. "Alright," I sighed. "You win. Let's go."

146

Annette had taken herself to one of the upstairs bathrooms. Helen knocked on the door softly.

"Yes?" Annette's terse voice was unmistakable.

"Hi. It's Helen, Jane's daughter. She's with me. I was wondering if you two could talk things through."

"Now why on earth would you think we'd want to do that?"

Poor Helen. She was no match for the wrath of Annette. She drew back uncertainly, then tapped again.

"I'm sorry Annette but I think it's silly to continue a quarrel that started two decades ago. It's obviously upsetting you both."

I heard the lock click. Oh no. The door opened, revealing a tear stained Annette.

"And what would you know about it?"

Helen looked taken aback for a moment, and then recovered her composure. "Nothing. I know nothing about it. But I know it's upsetting my mum. And you."

Annette turned to me. "And have you told her why I'm upset?"

I shook my head. "I'm sorry, Annette. I tried to stop her."

"That's always been your problem. You're weak."

I nodded. It was true.

Helen was becoming angry on my behalf.

"There's no need to be personal."

Annette laughed. "Personal? That's an interesting word to use."

Helen frowned. "What do you mean?"

I put my hand on Helen's arm. "Come on. Let's go."

Helen looked from one to the other of us. It seemed to be finally occurring to her that her foot was hovering over the edge of a minefield. And yet she continued to walk.

"Just tell me. Please."

147

Annette looked at me, allowing me the courtesy of one last appeal to Helen, but I knew there wasn't much point. I threw my hands in the air.

"There were some photos," said Annette, bitterly. "My husband is a fool. They were very compromising, from his perspective, but the woman involved was very careful not to show her face."

Helen looked at me. She had gone a shade paler as the truth began to take shape in her mind.

"She was asking for a large amount of money, which we didn't have. Luckily I found the pictures before James did anything even more stupid. Unfortunately it wasn't straightforward to work out which of his lovers had sent the pictures, but we traced the email address."

"I was silly," I said. "I thought I was in love with him. When he told me he was married I got angry." I turned to Helen. "Now can we leave?"

There was a noise behind us. "What's going on? My God, it's you!" James was standing at the top of the stairs. He was looking at Helen. She looked like she was about to faint.

"What on earth is going on?" asked Annette, looking from one face to another. "Do you two know each other?"

"Helen was one of my students," said James, weakly.

"I was only twenty," said Helen. "It was a stupid mistake. I thought it was in the past."

Annette was frowning, trying to rearrange all of the new information. "So *you* and James..." she began. But then, who—"

I closed my eyes. "I saw the email you sent to Helen on the family computer. So I looked back and found the ones she had sent to James. It was so stupid – she'd have been thrown off the course, and possibly have ended up with a criminal record. So I contacted James and told him to say it was me."

148

Annette looked at James. "That was why you didn't want to prosecute. You were protecting *her*." She pointed to Helen.

It was like some ludicrous tableau: an elf, Father Christmas and two old crackers having a row about some pornographic snaps from two decades ago. I started to giggle.

"Are you mad?" asked Annette.

Helen had gone from white to pink. "Let's go, Mum," she said.

"Finally!"

Later that evening I sat down in front of the fire with a large measure of scotch. I was still dressed as a Christmas cracker.

My laptop was open on my knee and the words were pouring from me. On the coffee table sat the invitation, recovered from the bin. Next to it was a bundle of letters, from James to me. Somehow it hadn't seemed important to go into that side of things, after everything with Helen. It would have felt like stealing her limelight, almost.

About the author
Karen Kendrick is a 40-year-old student and a published writer of short fiction. She knows she ought to have a real job by now but prefers writing stories to almost everything else.

Snow

Ian Inglis

Whenever the snow fell, he remembered a time from his childhood. Alastair Beech was fourteen years old when his parents decided to move from their three-bedroomed, terraced house near the town centre to a four-bedroomed, double-fronted, detached house in a new housing development on the site of an old convent just half a mile away. For Alastair, it was an uncontentious move. He welcomed the fact that the new house had a large garden, that his bedroom was twice the size of the one he was leaving, and although the journeys to and from school might take an extra few minutes he was relieved that he would be able to walk or cycle there with the same group of friends.

Within days of their house appearing on the market, his parents received an offer several thousand pounds above the price they had been told to expect. The prospective buyer was a young woman who was keen to complete the purchase as soon as possible. Following the advice of their estate agent, they immediately accepted her bid and looked around for somewhere to rent for several weeks until their new house was completed. They quickly found a furnished bungalow in a village two miles outside the town, placed their own furniture in storage, and moved in to their temporary home at the end of January.

For the next few weeks, Alastair was dropped off at school by his father on his drive to work, but on those days when their timings did not coincide he used the recently constructed Metro system which ran along the lines of the old suburban rail network and connected several of the small towns in the region. By and large he preferred this option. The journey was quick, the service was regular and reliable, and the large numbers of university students who used the system to travel between their outlying halls of residence and the town's central campus gave him the opportunity to eavesdrop on what he fondly imagined to be exciting and bohemian conversations. In addition, one of the stations on the route was close to St Dominic's School for Girls, and the crowded carriages provided opportunities for fleeting and unfamiliar physical contact with the opposite sex.

In many ways, he regarded their two months in rented accommodation as a holiday. He quickly grew to like the relative silence of the village over the constant drone of urban traffic to which he had been previously accustomed and discovered, almost by default, that he was spending more time on his school assignments and homework with a consequent increase in his grades. He also began to read some of the paperbacks that the bungalow's owner had left behind, by authors his parents and teachers had been encouraging for years – books by H. G. Wells, Aldous Huxley, George Orwell, and others. He felt comfortable with the new vocabularies, rhythms of speech and literary styles that he encountered, and asked his delighted parents to suggest other writers he might enjoy.

"Arthur Conan Doyle," his father advised.

"And Thomas Hardy," said his mother. "Start with *Tess Of The D'Urbervilles.*"

In early February, the country suffered a wave of blizzards blown furiously across the North Atlantic. Like most British families, Alastair and his parents had watched their television screens in fascination as reports of unprecedented snowfalls in North America brought many of the cities on the Eastern seaboard – New York, Boston, Washington – to a standstill. Although the storms had lost

151

much of their intensity when they hit Britain, the disruption was still considerable. Airports closed, cross-Channel ferry sailings were suspended, and rail services operated intermittent and unpredictable timetables. One overnight snowfall blanketed much of the country in an unrelenting layer of deep snow, and after several futile attempts to back his car out from the drive on to the main road, his father abandoned any hopes of driving into town.

"I'll work from home today," he said, "but you might be able to make it to school if the Metro's running."

Snow was still falling heavily as Alastair waited on the platform. However, the tracks were surprisingly clear and, after apologising profusely for the delay, the disembodied voice on the public address promised that a reduced service was in operation. For several minutes, the forty or fifty passengers on his side of the station stood facing a slightly smaller number on the opposite platform. Rueful comments about the weather passed within and between the two groups, and there were shouts and greetings over the ten-metres divide. Alastair spotted one of his new friends from the village and, without thinking about what he was doing, lobbed a snowball across at him. When it struck the boy on the shoulder, it produced a howl of surprise, followed by a spontaneous burst of applause from both groups. Alastair's initial embarrassment as the unexpected centre of attention disappeared when some of the university students standing near him encouraged him to throw another snowball.

"But this time," said a young woman in thick, multi-coloured, woollen leggings, "see if you can hit that guy with the red hat. I don't like the look of him!"

Swelling with pride, he drew careful aim at his target and narrowly missed. He was dusting the snow from his hands when the intended victim adopted a mock-ferocious pose and demanded to know who had thrown the snowball.

152

Before he could answer, the young woman, who evidently knew him, spoke up.

"I did! What are you going to do about it?"

"I'll show you what I'm going to do about it!"

He bent down to scoop up a handful of snow, but before he could straighten up, was struck on the side of his head by another snowball, and slipped over, losing his red ski-hat. Laughter rang out, and within seconds, snowballs were being flung across the tracks as more and more of the waiting passengers on both platforms joined the fray. Even those who declined to take direct action showed their approval and, for five, perhaps six minutes, the air was thick with reciprocal volleys of small, soft missiles that exploded into flurries of white powder. Alastair was astonished. Although he and his friends were well used to the multiple entertainments supplied by a snowy winter, the sight of men and women of his parents' age joyfully participating in an impulsive snowball fight, and urging others to do the same, was a revelatory experience. When a train eventually arrived to carry those on the opposite platform away from their brief battleground, there was an almost audible gasp of disappointment, and as it pulled away, he and the remaining passengers turned to face each other, red-faced with exertion, offering smiles and congratulations in a way he'd rarely seen before.

"That was fun," the woman in the leggings said to him. "We should do this every morning. And you started it!"

Two weeks later, the school held its annual short story competition. Those pupils who wished to enter were asked to write, in no more than 1000 words, a short story entitled *A Day To Remember*. Recalling and recording the events on the snow-covered platform as they happened, and adding a few invented details about those taking part, Alastair spent several days constructing and revising the story until it satisfied him. The results were posted on the school notice boards in the final week of the Easter term, grouped into three separate age categories. From the sixth form, the winner was Eleanor Marshall, a studious, earnest girl with a place waiting for her at Magdalen College, Oxford; from the middle school, the winner was Alastair; from the lower school, there were joint winners: Dipak Patel, a frighteningly intelligent boy who seemed to excel in all subjects, and Lizzie Fox, a noisy and extrovert girl with a stated ambition to go on the stage. And during the school assembly on the last day of term, the Headmaster announced that the overall winner of the short story prize (books to the value of £50-00) was Alastair Beech, whose entry he described as 'a combination of overt nostalgia and contemporary mischief, brimming with optimism and displaying a real talent for the use of language.'

And now the snow was falling again, in flurries that coated the Derbyshire countryside in a thin, milk-white dusting. In the forty years since that snowball fight had taken place, the winters had become milder and the snowfalls less frequent, but the significance he attached to *A Day to Remember* remained constant. Although the innumerable reports, proposals and evaluations he had been obliged to write throughout his long career in local government were routinely praised for their clarity, he regarded his schoolboy essay as the only authentic, the only worthwhile, piece of prose he had ever produced. He could almost recite it by heart. He remembered the morning at the Metro station in all its details, the clothes the people were wearing, the expressions on their faces, their shouts and cries and laughter.

The telephone rang. His wife, his two sons and their wives had travelled down to London ahead of him.

"What time's your train in the morning?" she asked.

"Seven o'clock. I'll be in London just after nine."

"Remember we're due at the Palace by eleven."

"I haven't forgotten, Geraldine. I'll come straight to the hotel. We'll have plenty of time."

There was a silence.

"I'm so proud of you," she said.

The letter from the Prime Minister's Principal Private Secretary had arrived at his home several months earlier.

I am asked by the Prime Minister to inform you that he has it in mind on the occasion of the forthcoming list of New Year Honours to submit your name to the Queen with a recommendation that she may be graciously pleased to approve that you be appointed a Knight Bachelor of the British Empire. Before doing so, the Prime Minister would be glad to be assured that this mark of Her Majesty's favour would be agreeable to you.

His first reaction was to refuse it, on the grounds that it represented the most hateful aspects of rank and privilege that permeated British society. But as he listened to Geraldine's protestations – it would mean so much to the family, he truly deserved it, it would be churlish not to accept it, it would provide a positive boost to a branch of government under siege – his opposition gradually dissolved and he wrote back to confirm that, yes, the knighthood would be agreeable to him. And here he was, with the investiture just a few hours away.

He lay in bed with the curtains open – he hated the dark – and watched the snow continue to fall. He saw himself again, the eager schoolboy standing on the platform, crouching down to gather a handful of snow, basking in the

155

praise of the girl in the coloured leggings, giving in to the feeling of pride that ran through him as he became the brief centre of attention. He saw himself in his bedroom, working tirelessly, writing and rewriting the story. He saw himself in the school hall, listening to the Headmaster announce the results of the short story competition. He saw his parents jump up from their chairs and rush towards him when he told them the news. He had never been so happy in his life.

When he woke, he saw that the snow had fallen throughout the night. Not enough to block the roads or delay the trains, but enough to enhance the wintry landscape. He made himself a light breakfast, and packed his overnight bag. The station was only a short walk away and there was no need to hurry. He went into the small study at the rear of the house, took out a creased, buff-coloured envelope and spread its contents on the desk. He held them gently, one by one: the typed pages held in place by a brass paperclip, the certificate bearing the school crest that confirmed his prize, a letter of commendation from the Headmaster, and the congratulatory card his parents had slipped under his bedroom door as he slept. He sat there, pages in hand, for some time, and wondered how many of his fellow passengers on the platforms that morning remembered the day. When the telephone interrupted his reading, he chose not to answer it, and when the ringing became incessant he put on his walking boots and set off along the bridleway that ran past the house and away from the town.

When he returned, it was mid-afternoon. A police car was waiting outside the front gate.

"Are you Alastair Beech?" the officer asked.

"Yes, I am."

"Are you alright, sir? Your wife telephoned us from London... she couldn't contact you and was rather worried."

"I'm fine. I've been for a walk. Now I've come back."

The officer looked at him, uncertainly.

"Would you like me to come inside with you, sir?" he asked.

"You can if you wish to. But there's really no need."

"Well... if you're sure. But I think it might be a good idea to call your wife. As I say, she seemed a little distressed."

"I will. I'll ring her now, as soon as I get inside. Thank you, officer."

The phone was ringing as he walked in through the door. He went to the kitchen and made a pot of tea. The ringing ceased, but started again almost immediately. He realised it would be pointless to ignore it.

"Alastair. For God's sake, what happened?"

"Hello, Geraldine. I went for a walk. It's a beautiful day up here," he said, calmly.

"Damn the weather! The investiture! Your knighthood! The Queen!"

"Oh, I don't think she'd notice my absence, do you? One missing person out of a few hundred?"

When she spoke again, the notes of concern in her voice were replaced by a bewildered anger.

"Have you taken leave of your senses? Or did you plan this? To hurt me? To deprive me of – of something? And the boys, too? They're devastated. What can we possibly have done to you to make you do this to us?"

"Geraldine, this has nothing to do with you," he said, evenly. "Or anyone else. The knighthood was awarded to me. For services to local government. Not to you. Why should you be upset?"

"It'll be rescinded, you know. They told me. They won't give you another chance to collect it," she said, bitterly.

"No, I don't imagine they will."

"Don't you care? Does it mean nothing to you? Do you know how embarrassed, how humiliated I was? I've had reporters ringing me. What do I tell people?"

He considered her question.

"You can tell them I forgot."

"Are you insane?! You don't forget that you're going to Buckingham Palace to be knighted by the Queen!" she cried.

"Then tell them it was because of the snow."

"The snow! What snow?! The roads are open, the trains are running. What are you talking about?"

"Snow," he said again.

"It's spite," she retaliated. "You know how much it meant to me. You did it deliberately. What you've done is despicable! You've insulted the Queen. You think this makes you look like a rebel? It makes you look like a fool! A selfish, thoughtless fool! You've disgraced us."

"Well, I'm sure I didn't mean to. Last night, you said how proud you are of me."

"I'm not proud. I'm ashamed. We were looking forward to such a lovely day. A day we'd never forget. None of us. A day we could look back on, for the rest of our lives. A day to remember."

As Geraldine predicted, the Palace rescinded his award. As the controversy provoked by his non-appearance spread, public opinion was polarised dramatically. Over the years, several people had died between the notification of their awards and the ceremony, some had returned their awards, others had discreetly refused when first approached – but nobody had ever agreed to accept a knighthood and then neglected to attend the ceremony. For some, it was a magnificent, admirable and bold rejection of an outdated system of patronage; for others, it was a dreadful and unforgivable affront to the dignity of the Queen herself; for a concerned few, it was evidence that either his memory or his mental state were defective. Some of the press – *The Express* and *The Mail* in particular – condemned it as a cheap publicity stunt. Some backbench Tories insisted he should be tried for sedition.

He declined all requests for interviews, and attempted to placate his exasperated family by assuring them that the media would soon find other incidents to exploit. He was right. Within a few days, a rent boy scandal at the Home Office provided the necessary respite, and the attention of the press shifted abruptly to more salacious events. Only once did the media manage to confront him directly. A memorable few seconds of TV footage showed Alastair and Geraldine door-stepped by a BBC camera crew: while she holds her hands over her face in despair, he speaks in measured and reasonable tones.

"Snow prevented me from making the journey from Derbyshire to London. While it may be true that, on the whole, I would prefer to be in the company of those who have refused or returned political honours than those who have accepted them, it was not ideology that led me to behave as I did. Not at all. It was snow."

About the author
Dr Ian Inglis is the author of seven books and more than sixty articles around topics within popular culture. He has taught in the Sociology departments at Leicester and Northumbria Universities, and has also worked as a reporter (in Stoke-on-Trent) and broadcaster (BBC Radio Newcastle).

http://ianinglis15.wix.com/website

The Annual General Meeting of the East Kent Macumba Society

Michele Sheldon

"They'll not be welcome here again," says Dad as we watch the convoy of cars speed away.

They approach the bend, their brake lights flashing red like devil eyes. I wish I could believe Dad but I can't. So I scrunch mine shut, willing our departing guests to crash and die. When I open them again, the cars have disappeared. Dad sighs heavily.

"Shall I start with the sitting room?" I ask.

"Most definitely not after last year's fiasco," says Dad. "You can start on the top floor. I've already had a quick look and it's not too bad, considering."

I drag my feet along the corridor, slowing outside the sitting room door, my hand reaching for the door knob.

"Ryan James!" says Dad, smacking my hand away. "We've got a lot to do before your mother's home."

"What if I find another?"

"Pick it up with a plastic bag and put it in the wheelbarrow at the bottom of the garden. I'll dispose of it as soon as I get a chance. Now, don't forget to wear gloves. Work your way around and we'll meet on the first floor."

"On my own? But that's six bedrooms... five en-suites."

"Less complaining and more cleaning, young man. Your mother's back at 6pm and you know how upset she got last time."

I stomp up the stairs. How could I forget? The screaming. The tears. Then the side effects from the anti-depressants.

"She shouldn't go on her stupid anniversary trip then should she?" I shout.

"Have some respect, Ryan James. Your mother needs a break after all her hard work," Dad yells up the stairs.

A bucket, mop, hoover and cleaning backpack are waiting for me on the first floor landing. I take a deep breath, wondering all sorts of bad thoughts. Like why Dad thinks it's okay to get his 14-year-old son involved with the East Kent Macumba Society but not his adult wife, who swans off every year to a spa with Auntie Sarah to mark Grandpa's death. And exactly what do aromatherapy massages and colonic irrigation have to do with remembering Grandpa anyway? Dad packs her off every year under the pretence of caring about Grandpa. But he knows she wouldn't put up with our guests for five minutes.

I don't expect the top floor to be too bad and find the first three rooms, two singles and a double, practically spotless. I'm guessing most of the mess is going to be on the first floor where all the drumming and shrieking was coming from.

But as I open the door to the master bedroom, I shrink back.

My eyes take in the sea of dead flowers scattered over the carpet and bed. I half expect the Bride of Frankenstein to stumble out of the en-suite. There's a horrible smell too. Like a public toilet. I pinch my nostrils shut, steeling myself for having to clear up other people's urine.

"Everything all right up there?" calls Dad.

"Piss and dead flowers," I shout.

"Language, Ryan James!"

I wrestle on the rubber gloves and snap the medical mask over my nose, feeling myself prickle with injustice: my language was nothing compared to what our guests got up to.

161

I begin with the flowers, picking up red and yellow rose petals and watch them crumble in my fingers, imagining our guests furtively harvesting dead flowers from cemeteries. Three large vases, I'd brought up the night before, are lying among the flowers, the yellow water creating multicoloured ponds in the swirly carpet, as well as the bad smell.

I strip the sheets. Apart from a few springy pubic hairs, I don't find anything else unpleasant. The bathroom too is surprisingly clean and I give it a quick going over with a cloth. I remember Mum's hysterical screaming and check behind the curtains and under the armchair, mini sofa and the bed. But all is clear and I take my cleaning equipment to the next room, a small double where the bedspread is cradling an imprint of two bodies. I clear several Brahama beer bottles from the sideboard and empty the dregs in the sink, wrinkling my nose at the yeasty stench as the golden liquid fizzes down the plug hole.

The next room is in much the same condition; one lone body shape in foetal pose imprinted on the bedspread. Although the bed hasn't been slept in, I strip it anyway as I know Dad will send me back if I don't. I use the mop to fish a pair of men's underpants from under the bed. They're emblazoned with a colour photo of the Sugar Loaf Mountain. I quickly shove them to the bottom of the bin bag, shuddering at the thought of Dad adopting them.

"Dad?" I shout as I walk down the stairs, trying to carry the hoover, mop, bucket and cleaning backpack at the same time.

It's too much. The hoover slips out of my hand and dramatically rolls down the stairs like it's a stunt hoover. I hurry after it but when I get to the bottom of the stairs, Dad is standing there dressed in Mum's pink cleaning pinny,

162

green rubber-gloved hands on hips, the hoover lying at his feet.

"I suppose it'd had enough of the mess and threw itself down the stairs?"

"It just slipped."

"Be more careful. Hoovers don't grow on trees, you know."

"Really? Not even suc-amore trees?"

Dad mock clips me round the ear.

"Come on! We haven't got time to mess around. I need some young legs to pop to the larder and fetch the stain remover. Blood's a bugger to get out of the curtains."

I jog downstairs and glance out of the larder window at the garden, remembering the night before. We were sleeping in Grandpa's old flat over the garage and while Dad snored the night away, I kept being woken up by shouting, drumming and a few screams of what I hoped was delight. I couldn't get back to sleep so I made myself a cup of tea and sat on the balcony with the man on the moon keeping me company. A few moments later, we watched the Brazilians spill out of the French windows onto the terrace, where after a lot of whispering, they gathered in a circle.

I'd quickly grabbed Grandpa's binoculars and watched a woman in her 60s, dressed in a long white robe and turban, waving her arms up and down. I recognised her from breakfast. She'd complained about her fried eggs being undercooked. I zoomed in as she went up to Nelson, the man who organised the AGM, and started wafting her hands around him as if he'd done a big stinky fart and she was trying to dissipate the smell. I felt embarrassed for him. But he just stood there, eyes closed, not at all fazed by being so publicly humiliated. She then moved onto Nelson's latest girlfriend, a twenty-something, olive-skinned woman with closely cropped bleached blonde hair, who again stood impassively as the woman went about her wafting.

But the weird thing was after she'd wafted five or six people, there was a strange greyish froth flowing from of her mouth and down her chin. By the time she'd finished wafting the entire circle of 30, her mouth was pouring with the stuff like she'd swallowed a box of washing powder. She then threw herself onto the lawn and rolled around as if her robes were on fire. I waited for someone to kneel down and help but they just stood there watching her convulsing as if such behaviour was an everyday occurrence. Perhaps it was in Brazil, but as we were on the outskirts of Dover, I thought I'd better wake Dad and call an ambulance. However, just as I was about to get up, she sat up, wiped the foam away with her robes and started chatting away as if nothing had happened.

I grab the stain remover and glance at the kitchen clock. We only had another three hours before Mum came home so I take the stairs two at a time, shouting for Dad.

All the bedroom and bathroom doors are closed. I knock on each just in case he's cleaning inside. But there's no sound of scrubbing or running water. Then, out of the corner of my eye, I spot a flash of fuchsia out of the landing window. It's Dad wheeling the barrow down to the end of the garden.

I sprint after him, and get there in time to see him tipping the barrow's contents onto the compost heap.

"Fetch the fork, will you son?"

I jog back with the fork and see Dad burying something with his foot.

"What was it?"

"You don't want to know."

"Not another one?"

164

"No," he says taking the fork from me and stabbing it into the compost.

"Just these."

He unearths two little sack cloth dolls, a single stitch for their eyes, mouth and nose, making them look more like evil cats than anything human.

"And the usual champagne bottles, burnt candles, and feathers."

"Feathers? From what?"

"I wonder?" he says, all sarcastic.

"Crow? Magpie?"

Dad shrugs and reburies the evil cats and I get my answer as I glimpse an oily black feathered head and beak.

I want to ask if he thinks that's where the blood on the curtains is from. But he's already wheeling the barrow back up the path.

My foot hovers over the mound.

"Ryan James," he growls.

I tear myself away. After he dumps the barrow at the door, we go straight to the first floor master bedroom.

"I won't be long. Why don't you start on the two bathrooms. I've checked them already. They just need a wipe round," he says, *Vanish* in one hand, closing the door with the other.

I put my ear to the door, listening to Dad grunting and cursing before shouting the familiar: "Never again!"

A few minutes later, Dad emerges and we head to room 10, a large double.

The stench of stale river water hits us as soon as he opens the door. It smells like the trout Uncle Tom sometimes brings when he visits.

"Jesus," says Dad, looking down at the bed. "It's soaked through. The mattress will be ruined; there's no way they're getting their deposit back."

"What the hell were they doing?"

"Nelson said they were doing the dolphin thing this year but I thought he meant it figuratively…"

"Figuratively?"

"I didn't think he actually believed they could summon the spirit of an Amazonian dolphin and do it…"

"Do what?"

"You know. They do it," he said nodding his head at the bed. 'The dolphin does the… business with the ladies."

"A dolphin? That's disgusting!"

"It's not an actual dolphin. It's the spirit of a dolphin."

"It's still disgusting."

"This is disgusting," says Dad sniffing around the bed like a dog.

He pulls back the soggy velvet bedcover to reveal a saturated mattress, sprouting patches of bright green algae fur.

I clamp my hand over my nose.

"You know I saw them outside last night."

Dad looks up at me.

"Hope they didn't see you spying on them. That's in the contract. No prying, taking photos or asking questions."

"I wasn't prying. I couldn't sleep. That women who always complains. She had foam…"

"You saw the cleansing then," interrupts Dad, scooping handfuls of algae into the bucket. "I pay a fortune for a therapist, they pay a fortune for an annual spiritual cleanse."

"If Mum knew what was going on… knew that you were renting this place out to a voodoo society."

"It's not voodoo. It's macumba."

"I've Googled it, Dad. It's pretty much the same thing."

"It's nothing like it," says Dad, jabbing a slimy green forefinger at me. "Now don't you dare say anything!"

"I wouldn't, not after last year. I wouldn't mind but I was the one who found it. What about the effect on me? I still can't get that image out of my head. It looked just like Squeaker."

"Squeaker died when you were seven."

"I was 11. He had the same sweep of hair and centre parting," I say. "Why do you think Mum was so upset? She'd hand-reared him."

"Stop for a moment, Ryan and think. How could it have been Squeaker? He was a brindle. That one was ginger," says Dad yanking back the sheets. "Help me with these."

I stomp to the other side of the bed and tug back the soggy sheets, remembering how I'd spotted its glassy eyes gazing up at me from underneath the piano stool as I sat on the sofa watching TV. In hindsight, I should have ignored it until Mum had left the room. But I couldn't help glancing at it. Wondering if it really was Squeaker back from his grave with a new hairdo? Or had a fox dug him up and Bernard, our cat, brought him in? When I looked closer I realised, of course, it couldn't be him. He'd been dead for four years. He'd be a skeleton, whereas this one looked very much in rude health before our guests had cut off its head.

Dad had managed to convince Mum the head belonged to an obese squirrel we'd seen Bernard eyeing up as it struggled to climb the willow tree. However, he couldn't quite so easily explain how Bernard had managed to get hold of the bloody pile of entrails she'd found under one of the beds.

Dad shoves the mattress up against the wall.

"We'll leave it overnight. Say one of the guests spilled some tea and then you came along and accidently knocked a bucket of water all over it…"

"Why me? Why can't you…" I begin to say as the phone in reception rings.

167

"Get that, will you. It's probably your mum, letting us know she's about to leave."

"But…?"

"It's okay, don't worry. I'll finish off up here," says Dad, patting the mattress with a towel.

I run down the stairs and throw myself at the phone.

"Hello, Mum?"

A familiar voice greets me.

I place my hand over the receiver and shout up the stairs.

"Dad!"

He's already half way down and when he's at the bottom, I whisper: "Are you going to tell him where he can stick his AGM?"

Dad nods and takes the receiver before shooing me back upstairs. I linger halfway up, out of sight but still in earshot.

"Hello… Yes, quite a bit. A new mattress, new curtains and possibly a new carpet in room 10. We're looking at about £2,000 over the deposit."

I strain my ears waiting for Dad to tell them.

"That's very generous. Yes, you can pay it directly into the account," he says.

I bristle at Dad doing his fake 'I'm such a great host' laugh.

"No worries… Same time next year, you say? Well, I'm not sure if we're already booked… Dover Taxis have been on the phone about a dinner and dance… Oh… really? That's very tempting but I'm not sure I can cancel. They've already paid a hefty deposit. Let me just see what I can do."

I hear the diary pages rustling and cross my fingers tightly.

"Ah, yes, that's all booked for you… And you, Nelson. De nada!"

The end

About the author

Michele Sheldon's short stories have won and been short listed for many prizes.

They have also been published in several anthologies including both volumes of *Stories for Homes*, and magazines including *Rosebud, Storgy, Here Comes Everyone, Kent Life* and *Woman's Weekly*.

She co-hosts live lit events with Hand of Doom Productions and her first play, *Flagpole*, was performed at Dover Castle as part of the Marlowe Theatre's WW1 project.

The Bogeyman

Steve Wade

Jamie was now in the bogeyman's house. The bogeyman had a wife. And there was a boy. The boy was smaller than Jamie and crazy. He had long hair like a girl's. Jamie had heard the boy laughing and talking to himself during the night. Jamie had been locked into a room next to the crazy boy's. Morning time now, and the crazy boy wanted to play with him. He called Jamie by a different name: 'Wiley'. But the bogeyman called him 'Riley'.

"Pa, Pa," the boy called out. "Wiley won't play diggers with me." He ran out the door into the scary place where the bogeyman hid in the shadows.

Through the open door came the cold. The cold had fangs. And the skeleton hanging in the porch rattled.

"Riley," the skeleton said. And Jamie felt in his tummy that feeling he sometimes got when he needed to go to the toilet. "Riley," the skeleton said again, only this time it was the bogeyman stepping into the house. He spoke with the skeleton's voice.

It's okay, son," the bogeyman said. "No one is going to hurt you." White hairs grew down from inside his nostrils.

Jamie grasped the curtain, and pulled it round him the way he often pulled his Dracula cape over his shoulders in his own house.

"What are you doing, the two of you, to the frightened lamb?" he heard a woman's voice go. The bogeyman's wife: the woman who had spoken to him on the street when he was trick-or-treating – the woman who had taken him to the bogeyman's car.

"Shona, please, the boys were just getting to know each other again," he heard the bogeyman say.

Back came the curtain. Gently.

"There. There," she said. "My little lamb, lost for too long in the wilderness. Come with me," she said.

Jamie took her hand. It felt cold and shiny. She took him upstairs. Where they'd brought him last night.

Upstairs smelled the way his puppy smelled in the rain. And he couldn't see properly.

"Turn on the lights," he said. "I'm scared."

"That's okay, love," she said. "There's no one here wants to harm you. If you're good."

Jamie pressed in closer to her as they moved to the open door at the end of the shadowy landing. She bent forward and into him, her face over his shoulder. The smell of sugared tea from her mouth, like his mama's sweetened smell.

"Now," she said. "Do you remember this, Riley? Your room – yours and Dale's."

In the bedroom were two beds, one on top of the other. The beds were blue with blankets of blue and white squares, some red. Attached to the sides of the beds, a wooden ladder.

"Go ahead, love," she said.

He climbed up the ladder. On his knees in the bed, Jamie looked around him. There were soldiers on a press, four or five, wearing red coats and big black hats. And, on the shelf on the wall beside him, a robot, which he picked up.

The woman laughed. "Oh," she said. "Riley, would you look at this."

She held up to him a picture she'd taken from the wall.

Jamie looked at the picture. Two boys. Older boys. He went back to tinkering with the robot.

"Who's that?" she said, her voice wrapped up in a smile. She tapped on the glass covering the picture.

171

Jamie glanced at the photo again. He shrugged his shoulders.

"It's you, you little rascal. You and Dale, on your birthday it was. Just before you and Dale..." She didn't continue. Her face changed. She turned from him. Jamie thought he heard her crying.

Footsteps clopping like a small horse outside the bedroom jerked Jamie's head towards the door. The crazy boy, his face the face of an angry puppet, his eyes growing bigger, madder, while locked onto the robot in Jamie's hands.

"That's mine," he said, and he charged at Jamie.

"Wait, wait," the woman said. She caught the boy in mid-run, her hands under his armpits. She did a twirl with him in her arms.

The boy struggled and squirmed to get free.

"My robot," he said. "It's mine."

"Ah ah," the woman said. "Now Dale. You be a good boy. You know what happens when you're naughty."

The boy quietened. And the way he dropped his head into his chest, his eyes looking at the ground, reminded Jamie of his family's pet Cocker Spaniel when Jamie's daddy shouted at it because the puppy was being a 'scallywag'.

"That's it," she said. "Now, nobody's going to hurt you if you're good. You just do as you're told. Your pa won't always be around to stop you getting punished when you don't do what your mama says."

She placed the boy on the floor. He didn't move.

"Okay, you two," the woman said. "You know what day today is, don't you?"

The crazy boy's face changed. "It's nicnic day," he said. He didn't look crazy anymore.

"That's right, sweetheart. Picnic day."

172

The crazy boy jumped up and down, flapping his arms like a chicken.

Jamie climbed down off the top bunk. He didn't know why. He just did.

"Right," the woman said. She pulled open the doors of a big wardrobe.

That's when the crazy boy spat into Jamie's face. Jamie smelled the yucky sticky spit. And he spat back.

A red flash exploded across Jamie's eyes. And he was on the floor, the woman standing over him, her mouth twisted. She pointed her finger at him.

"No. You don't hit your little brother. Never. You hear me?"

Jamie's cheek stung, the way it had that afternoon one time when he played football too long in the burning sun. The woman bent over closer to him, her hand raised behind her.

"Do you hear me?" she said.

She'd hit him, he only then realised. He heard himself wailing like a baby. Though he nodded his head furiously, so she wouldn't smack him again.

"Crybaby," she said. "You're nothing but a…"

"What're you doing to him?" the figure that'd stepped into the room asked. The bogeyman.

"Nothing," the woman said. Now she was smiling and moving her arms about and turning and twisting her hands in the air. "He slipped. The robot. He fell over it."

"Quit dancing," the bogeyman said. "I swear to God, Shona. You need help."

"Don't," she said. "Don't you say that about me." She jumped at the bogeyman.

"Okay, okay," he said. He held up his arms and backed away from her. He looked scared. "Just control yourself, all right? You're frightening him." He left the room.

"Right," she said. "Time to change our clothes, boys."

The crazy boy made a shriek. Next he was kicking off his shoes, stepping out of his jeans, and pulling off his T-shirt.

"Okay, the woman said to the crazy boy. She handed him what looked like a girl's blue dress. "Your favourite."

The boy pulled it on over his head, but got his arms tangled.

"Here, silly," the woman said. "You're all twisted. It's back to front." She helped him.

Now, with his long hair and the dress, the boy looked just like a girl. He pushed his feet, one at a time, into his runners, whose laces he'd left tied when he'd taken them off.

"This is your one, Riley," the woman said. She held up a girl's dress by the shoulders – a brown one.

Jamie shook his head.

"Take it," she said. "Put it on the way Dale did. Good boy."

"I want my mama," he said, after drawing in breath.

"I'm here, love," the woman said. "Mama's here." She laughed. But her laugh was scary. Like a witch's. And Jamie felt a hot, wet sensation in his pants, which quickly turned cold. He needed to go to the toilet. His tummy hurt. So he thought he'd do another little bit of wee-wee to stop the pain. But once he started, he couldn't stop.

"Mama. Mama. Look. Wiley's done a pee-pee," the crazy boy said. He pressed his hand over his mouth and sniggered.

Jamie reversed to a dark corner at the end of the bunk beds. His light-coloured chinos – his favourite pants – now had a dark stain in the shape of a squish painting. It looked as if he had spilled a cup of juice into his lap.

"You dirty thing," the woman said.

174

Jamie felt her big man's hand grabbing him by the arm. She squeezed too hard, and dragged him into the bathroom.

The next thing Jamie realised was she'd pushed him into the shower, without taking off his clothes, and hot water was splashing down on him. He couldn't breathe.

He screamed. She shouted. Big hands pushing him, tugging at his jumper, and opening his belt. The bar of soap she rubbed against his body felt hard and cold. His mama always used a sponge.

"Lift up your arms," she said. "Up. Up."

Jamie did. And he did everything else she told him to do. He even tried to dry himself with the towel she gave him, while she left the bathroom to get clean clothes. He'd never used a towel before. His mama always dried him.

"Here, give it here," she said. She snatched the towel from him.

When she'd finished drying him, she put some of the white powdery stuff under his arms – the same stuff Jamie's mama used.

"Now," she said. She was scrunched down. Her cranky eyes the eyes of a seagull. In the corners of her mouth full of big yellow teeth, bubbly white spit. He thought she might bite him. But her turned-down mouth twisted upwards into a smile. And she leaned forward and kissed him. "Let's get you dressed."

This time Jamie allowed her to put the dress on him without a fuss.

"Good girl," she said. And now we need something for that pretty little face of yours.

He stopped himself from protesting that he wasn't a girl.

In the car on the way to the picnic, the woman, the crazy boy and the bogeyman sang songs. The car was the same big black one he'd been in the night before. He'd been trick-

or-treating with some friends from his street and a few of their mammies and daddies. The bogeyman's wife had stopped him in the street outside somebody's house. There she'd spoken to him for a bit, asking him questions: What was his name? Where did he go to school? How old was he? And were his parents with him while trick-or-treating? When he told her they were at home, she said that his little pals and the grown-ups had moved on, and that they'd better 'scoot after' them. But, the thing is she'd taken him by the hand and turned around and gone the wrong way. A shortcut, she told him. They were taking a shortcut. The next thing he knew was a huge hand over his nose and mouth, the smell of corned beef, and being picked up and put into the black car.

"Quick. Quick," the woman had said to the bogeyman.

In the back of the car, Jamie saw the crazy boy for the first time. While the bogeyman held him down below the seats, and the bogeyman's wife drove, he felt the sound of the engine in his tummy. The whole time on that drive that seemed to last forever, the crazy boy stared down at him, laughing, and he kept prodding him with his fingers.

Nobody held Jamie down now. The bogeyman drove the car and the woman sat beside him. The crazy boy stood up on the floor in the back seat, his hands on the front seats. Sometimes he took the woman's long grey hair in his hands, asked her for the brush, and brushed it.

In between songs, the woman said that being dressed as girls was a game. When they got to the park, Dale and Riley were going to play girls' games.

"I want the pram," the crazy boy said. "Mommy, I want the pram. The pram." His arms were raised and he shook his hands like he was trying to fly.

"Yes, love," she said. "But you have to let Riley play with some of the other things."

176

Jamie said he wanted to play 'Secretary'. This was a game he and his sister played together.

The woman twisted round to him from the front seat. "Wonderful," she said. She clapped her hands and asked him how you played the game.

Jamie explained that the secretary talks on the phone to someone with a pain in his tooth. He opened his mouth and touched one of his back teeth.

"A toothache," the woman said. "Oh, Riley, you always were such a clever boy. Good girl."

The bogeyman laughed.

"And, and," Jamie said, "Barbara's the secretary and I get to be the dentist."

The woman's happy face changed to the witch's face. "Who's Barbara?"

"Barbara's my sister. She's the secretary," he repeated. "And I'm the dentist."

The woman shook her head. "No. No. Dale is your sister. Okay? Dale. Say it. Say 'Dale is my sister'."

By now, Jamie was learning that the woman said strange things. Just like his grandad. His mammy and daddy told him lots of times how his grandad wasn't well. They said that when people aren't well, they sometimes say and do strange things.

"Dale is my sister," he said.

The woman's witch-face went away.

Jamie recognised the park. He had been there before with his mammy, his daddy, and his sister. They'd been to the zoo. But he didn't tell the woman and the bogeyman.

When they'd finished the picnic of crisps, and small pink cakes with cherries on top, the woman said she had an idea. She gave them each a phone, her own and the bogeyman's. Jamie was the secretary, she decided. She told him to go over to the trees. She pointed at them. And his office was inside. He was to wait there until Dale called to make an appointment.

The forest was dark and cool. But Jamie didn't feel frightened. The number. His mammy and daddy had taught him to remember the number. 01 came first. He remembered. Then there was his age, five. The next was the amount of eggs in two egg baskets. That's when the phone rang.

"Hello, mammy," he said.

"Hi," the voice said. And it laughed. The crazy boy. "I'm not mammy. I have a..." Jamie heard the woman speaking in the background. "Toothache," she said. "I have toothache."

"Okay," Jamie said. "Can you come in tomorrow? The dentist can see you tomorrow." He pressed the red button, while the crazy boy was repeating his question to the woman.

He tried again to remember the number his mammy and daddy told him to ring if he was ever lost or felt frightened. They told him to ring it if there was someone, a policeman maybe, with a phone. He pressed in the numbers he knew. There was also a number from a song. Two numbers – and then there were the days in the week. Altogether, there were ten numbers. Digits, his daddy called them. He counted them on the screen – ten. He pressed the dial button. It rang once before his mammy answered.

"Hello," she said. "Who is this?" She was crying.

"Hi Mammy."

"Jamie. Jamie. Oh my God, it's Jamie. Where..." And then his daddy was talking.

"Jamie. Listen to me."

"Daddy," he said. "I'm at the zoo."

"The zoo," his father repeated. "Quick, call the police. He's at the zoo."

178

Jamie knew his daddy was talking to his mammy. He felt frightened.

"Jamie," his father continued. "Listen carefully, son. Are you inside the zoo or outside?"

Jamie told him he was at the big chimney thing. The boot.

"He's at the Wellington monument," his father's said. "Jamie, are you by yourself or with somebody. Who's with you?"

The crazy boy was running across the grass towards Jamie's office in the forest.

"The bogeyman," Jamie said. "And the crazy boy. He has a toothache."

"Okay," his father said. "Is the bogeyman there now? Are you alone? Can they hear you?"

"They're on the steps," he said. "I'm in the trees. It's a pretend office."

"Good. Now listen. Don't tell anyone you were talking to me. And you weren't talking to mammy either. Okay?"

"Yeah," Jamie said. "Okay, Daddy."

"We'll be there soon, son. Good boy. Turn off the phone now. And remember, do not tell them we were talking, Okay?"

"Okay. Bye, Daddy."

The crazy boy burst through the trees. He said he was to come back for ice cream.

His ice cream was already melting down the cone when he got back to the steps. Jamie's mammy always gave him a tissue, but he was afraid to ask for one.

When the car with a siren arrived, he'd long since finished the ice cream, and they were packing up to go home.

"Bee-baw-bee-baw," the crazy boy went.

And then Jamie saw his daddy's silver car. Out of it

179

jumped his mammy and daddy. But there were policeman in front of them. They had their arms stretched out.

"It's him," his mammy shouted. "Jesus Christ, it's my baby."

The bogeyman had picked up Dale and was running into the forest. The policemen shouted and ran after him. The bogeyman's wife stayed where she was, sitting on a blanket, with her head in her hands. Everything happened very quickly after that.

His mammy and daddy were hunched down beside him. A crowd had gathered. Everywhere policemen. His mammy's arms wrapped around him so tightly, he couldn't breathe. She was crying. She smelled like flowers. And her wet face wet his face. And she kissed him, and kissed him, and kissed him, and kept on crying and kissing him and saying his name and kissing him and crying.

About the author

A prize nominee for the PEN/O'Henry Award, 2011, and a prize nominee for the Pushcart Prize, 2013, Steve Wade's fiction has been published widely in print and in digital format. His work has won awards and been placed in prestigious writing competitions, including being shortlisted in the Francis McManus Short Story Competition, 2013. His unpublished novel On *Hikers' Hill* was awarded First Prize in the UK abook2read Literary Competition, December 2010.

www.stephenwade.ie

The Flaw

Stuart Larner

It was not until Francesca had brought the antique bowl back to her shop and inspected it beneath her lamp that she saw the crack.

She swore at herself. How could she, the owner of one of the premier antiques shops in town, have spent five hundred on such a bowl when its value was now probably a fraction of that? She noticed that the date marks on the bowl were letters, whereas they were usually coded dots for that period of Royal Worcester. Yet, the depiction of the apples, pears and plums was so lifelike that she could almost pick them from the bowl surface and eat them.

She knew that she should not sell it at a high price knowing it had a flaw. Later discovery by an expert would publicly taint her reputation as surely as the crack marred the bowl. Then she thought of her long-planned cruise holiday, and what might happen if she had insufficient funds to cover it when the time came.

She wondered how many of her customers would see the crack in her dimly-lit shop if she could barely see it. If a tourist whom she would never see again bought it, there might not be any comeback as it would have been offered on an as-found basis. She dared to put it in the window at eleven hundred.

Many passers-by stopped to gaze at it through the window, but none offered to buy it. In her mind each aborted purchase was a punishment for displaying it at such a high price, and each day that the bowl remained unsold in her window was a glaring reminder to her of her deception. Over the weeks she reluctantly reduced the price, and this lessened her guilt. Then, just as she was closing early one day, a distinguished-looking man in a suit and bowtie appeared.

"A genuine Royal Worcester bowl," assured Francesca. "Some of them go for thousands. A bargain at six hundred."

"Royal Worcester? It's beautiful. I live in Worcester, and I am thinking of running for parliament. It would be important to show that I cared about the area and had links with the city. But I really wouldn't pay more than four hundred for a fruit bowl."

"I can't take anything less than five fifty for such an important piece."

"What? Five fifty?" He suddenly grabbed the bowl and waved it. "Too much. What about four fifty?"

Francesca was afraid that he might damage it and reddened. "Well, f-five w-would be my best price. It's genuine, all right. If that's what you're worried…"

"I'll take your word for it," he interrupted, opening his coat with the hand still precariously holding the bowl, and reaching inside for his wallet with the other. "Five it is. Wrap it up."

"Thank you, Mr Brotherington," said Francesca with a cold smile. She liked to remember people's names from their credit cards in case they were famous or there were later problems. She had not heard of him, but she thought that from his conceitedness he might soon attract fame of one sort or another.

He left the shop smiling.

A few months later on a Sunday evening, Francesca poured her usual glass of quality sherry from her crystal decanter, kicked off her fluffy slippers, rested her bare feet upon a footstool, and turned on the television to watch her favourite antiques programme.

"For this week's programme we visited the historic city of Worcester," said the voice-over.

Francesca raised her eyebrows.

The camera panned the crowded hall as the voice-over continued. "We saw an intriguing array of oak furniture, carriage clocks, and rococo French bureaux with hidden compartments for love letters, but we were very excited by this rare object."

Francesca sat bolt upright in her chair as Brotherington appeared on the screen alongside the bowl which was being cradled in an expert's worshipping hands.

"Well, this is, of course, a Royal Worcester fruit bowl, painted by the great Octar Copson. Tell me, how did you come by it?" the expert asked.

Francesca froze with her glass before her lips.

Brotherington took a breath and spoke with faultless ease. "Well, my great-grandfather was a notable dignitary and a very important man in Worcester and he knew Copson. Copson gave him this bowl as a wedding gift, and it's been passed down through my family ever since. So you see that's how I am connected to the great Octar Copson, the Master of Worcester."

Francesca took a large gulp of her sherry in disbelief.

"Yes, of course, nineteenth century," the expert nodded. "A perfect basis for provenance and – if I may say so – a demonstration of your important link to the city."

Brotherington beamed.

Francesca scowled.

"Now this brings me to a remarkable fact about this piece of classical pottery," the expert continued. "And that is – the date marks. You realise that the Copson bowls that the world knows were painted after the famous Pershore Plum plate of 1880 and most have coded dots as date marks. This has letters – indicating that it was perhaps made

183

earlier, possibly as a prototype piece. For that curiosity reason, it is extremely collectable and would be worth between two and three thousand."

Francesca's feet knocked over her footstool as she jumped up in alarm.

Brotherington flushed, pulled at his collar and bowtie, and tilted his head as if for a portrait photographer.

"However…" the expert got out his magnifying glass. "There's a crack in it which reduces the value quite considerably. I'm afraid it's only worth a thousand."

Francesca sat slowly back down again.

"Crack! Where?" yelled Brotherington. He grabbed the bowl. The expert, who had been holding a pose for the camera, let go of the bowl under the surprising force of Brotherington's wrench. The suddenness of the release took Brotherington by surprise and the bowl flew from his hands. It smashed into pieces on the floor.

About the author
Stuart Larner is a chartered psychologist. Besides writing for scientific journals, he has written articles, poems, stories, and pieces for the stage. He has published four books: *Jack Daw and the Cat*; *Guile and Spin*; *Hope: Stories from a Women's Refuge* (with Rosie Larner, collectively as Rosy Stewart); and *The Car*. He has stories in Bridge House Anthologies 2016 and 2017.

See his blog http://stuartlarner.blogspot.co.uk.

The mePhone

Boris Glikman

One day a new type of phone that you could use to call yourself appeared on the market. All one had to do was dial a certain number and one would be connected straight away with oneself. The quality of the reception was so good that the voice on the other end of the line sounded as if it was coming from the very same room.

Inevitably, there was some initial apprehension about using this phone, for no one quite knew what kind of a response they would receive when they rang themselves out of the blue for the very first time. What if their unexpected call was considered to be an impertinent and unforgivable invasion of privacy? Eventually, these fears subsided as most found that they were greeted with warmth and enthusiasm and their calls were seen as a pleasant surprise.

People rushed to purchase this new invention, which was marketed under the brand name "mePhone". Suppliers could not keep up with the demand and there were ugly scenes as customers fought amongst themselves for the last available mePhone.

The advertising campaign for the mePhone was built around the slogan: "With the mePhone, there'll be no more me-phoniness or lying to yourself!" and for once the reality corresponded exactly to the promotional claims, as it truly was a unique invention the likes of which had never been seen before.

For the mePhone to work properly certain procedures, as set out in the Owner's Manual, had to be followed. First, the reception only worked in particular areas, access to which required an extra fee. Second, there was a strict time limit on how long you could spend speaking with yourself.

And third, when using the mePhone, one had to wear special apparel that was sold separately from the phone. Also, the cost of a call was outrageously expensive, although some enterprising phone companies, hoping to capitalise on the popularity of the mePhone, for a while only charged a local call rate.

The high charge for using a mePhone was partly due to the technical complexities involved in establishing a connection, for there were many impostors who pretended, for their own twisted and devious reasons, to be the voice of your true inner self. Thus, a lot of specialist expertise was required to connect you to the real you. The biggest technical problem to overcome, however, was how to avoid getting a busy signal when calling yourself, for if you were calling yourself then that meant you were already on the phone and thus your line must, ipso facto, be engaged. So it was an astounding technological achievement that the creative wizards behind the mePhone were able to somehow surmount this seemingly unresolvable paradox and allow people to get through to themselves. How it was actually done remained, for obvious reasons, a tightly guarded industrial secret. There was speculation that it involved utilising the Many Worlds quantum theory, so that by using the mePhone a person was connected to themselves in another parallel Universe.

However, the steep costs and other inconveniences were more than outweighed by the benefits one gained from having a good chat with oneself, for no one ever had the time to stop and take a good, honest look at their lives. Everyone was always rushing about, preoccupied with the mundane details of existence, trying to silence the nagging questions of whether or not they were happy with their lives and if they were being true to their inner selves. The users of the mePhone could now catch up with all the things in their lives they never had the chance to think about before, to find out the vital news that fell by the wayside as they were speeding along the road of life.

Conversation flowed easily as people found that talking with yourself was a lot like talking to an old confidant you hadn't seen for a long time and with whom the most intimate matters could be discussed candidly. Not infrequently tears were shed as truths one had been hiding from oneself for many years were revealed and conveyed in forthright terms. Conversations gained a confessional aspect, as darkest secrets and problems known only to oneself were divulged openly over the phone lines. Quite often, surprises were lying in store as people discovered what they were really feeling inside. At other times, the voice on the other end of the line would remind you of your long-neglected dreams, of desires and needs you had suppressed for far too long. Many found out they weren't really happy in their places of employment. Some realised they had fallen out of love a long time ago. Others saw for the first time that they had deluded themselves as well as others into believing they had reached fulfilment. Quite a few recognised that they had become so comfortable with being miserable and disenchanted that they shrank back in fear when contentment appeared to be within easy reach. And so it was an enlightening and cathartic experience to be able to have a deep and meaningful talk with oneself.

Naturally, some were reluctant to use the mePhone, afraid of the frank and unvarnished truths that they might reveal to themselves, too scared to ask themselves what it is that they really wanted from life and what would make them happy. They had an instinctive aversion to self-exploration and self-discovery, due to their fear of what they might find lurking in the shadows and depths of their souls. Or, perhaps, they were afraid of what they might *not* find there, given how easy it was to deceive oneself that one possessed undiscovered talents and untapped potential hiding somewhere within. And so these people avoided using the mePhone, for it had an unparalleled ability to demolish all the delusions with which they comforted themselves throughout their lives.

The mePhone became so popular that it turned into an obsession for some users who spent all their time listening to and talking with themselves, finding it to be much more satisfying and fascinating than conversing with others.

Alas, for an unfortunate few, no matter how many times they tried, they just could not reach themselves on their mePhones; either no one would pick up the mePhone on the other end or if it was picked up, it would be hung up as soon as one said "hello" to oneself. In some cases, a connection could not be established due to the line being broken or the number always being engaged or disconnected.

In a way, it was a brilliant invention – both going against the zeitgeist, for the predominant trend was to avoid introspection, yet, at the same time quite fitting for the times, for everyone was communicating endlessly via all kinds of phones, having superficial conversations via texting, emails, tweets and instant messaging, yet never once listening to their own true inner voice. Consequently, all connection to oneself was lost and people were living unauthentic lives, deaf and blind to their own feelings, needs, desires. With the mePhone, one was able to satisfy the insatiable need for electronic devices and yet, at the same time, engage in deep, invaluable introspective explorations, analyses and discoveries.

The world became a better, happier place because of the mePhone as people at last began to be true to their own selves, for they knew they could no longer get away with lying to themselves. The way life had been before the mePhone was just a distant, faded memory and no person could imagine ever being without one.

About the author
Boris Glikman is a writer, poet and philosopher from Melbourne, Australia. The biggest influences on his writing are dreams, Kafka, Dali and Borges. His stories, poems and non-fiction articles have been published in various online and print publications, as well as being featured on national radio and other radio programs.

Timothy and Pandora's Box

Dawn Knox

Alice poked her finger through the hole in the tablecloth and wiggled it.

"The moths in this house must have teeth like rats."

Her friend Margery, who was sitting next to the fire, looked up from her knitting, "It probably *was* a rat. I told you when you put it away you ought to wash it first. Vermin are attracted to food—"

"Well, thank *you* for stating the obvious! And may I remind you, the washing machine isn't padlocked. You could get up off your rather considerable backside and use it yourself. I don't know why I have to do everything round here!"

"Oh dear," said Margery, "someone's a crosspatch this afternoon."

"Crosspatch indeed! And if I am, I have good reason! It makes my hackles boil to think I've got to put up with the little monster and his wife all evening. *And* feed them both."

"Blood, dear. Blood boils… hackles rise. You've mixed your metaphors."

"Rubbish! You can't boil blood."

"No, dear. Well, I get your drift, but calling him a monster? That's a bit harsh. He's your only nephew, and to be fair, you haven't gone to a lot of trouble. Tinned soup to start, tinned meat stew for the main course followed by tinned sponge pudding. Not an ambitious menu. It hardly tested your imagination or your culinary skills. The only challenge was to the tin opener."

"I'll have you know the rather considerable squeezing and twisting involved in opening all those tins played havoc with the arthritis in my wrists."

"Well, I've always said you should take up knitting. *Use it or lose it*, I say. My wrists are perfectly fine." She put the knitting in her lap and demonstrated by rotating her hands first one way, then the other, "See?"

"I would think their flexibility owes more to the fact you never actually do anything around the house, than that you spend all day knitting. And may I say, I never see any finished articles, for all the time you spend waggling your needles."

"Shall I knit you a tablecloth, dear? It'll have fewer holes than that one."

Alice huffed as she laid the cloth on the table, "I shall simply place table mats in strategic places. No one will notice the holes. And if Timothy and his new wife spot them, they'll simply think I've fallen on hard times and can't afford a new one. That'll put a spoon in their works."

"Spanner."

"Spoon! Spanner! Whatever!"

"You're acting as though they're going to come round and mug you, dear. They're only going to try to impress you in the hope you'll leave them everything in your will."

"I'd rather leave it to the cats' home."

"You hate cats, dear."

"Dogs' home then."

"You hate dogs. Is there such a place as a retirement home for pandas? You like pandas. You could always try that."

"Retirement home for pandas!" Alice muttered as she picked up the table mats she'd been laying on the table.

"I thought you were going to cover the holes with those mats," said Margery.

"The holes are all in the wrong places. It looks like I've thrown the mats up in the air and left them wherever they landed. And anyway, I'm rather liking the plan to convince the scroungers I've lost my fortune."

"*Scroungers* is a bit harsh, isn't it?"

191

"Not at all. Timothy might be my only brother's son but he's never taken the slightest interest in me before."

"Well, he did come round just after last Christmas, didn't he?"

"Only because I didn't sign the cheque I sent him. As soon as I did, he was gone."

"He soon came back when he noticed you'd signed it *Ebenezer Scrooge.*"

"Honestly, Margery, is it too much to ask one's only nephew for a little bit of consideration and time. I don't want to feel I'm just dotty, rich, old Auntie Alice. It's like everyone's waiting for me to drop my clogs."

"Pop your clogs, dear. Or drop off the perch. I don't think you can drop clogs."

"Of course you can. Don't be ridiculous. You can drop anything."

"If you say so, dear… Now, it's just a suggestion, but why don't you have a nap before they come? You seem to be getting rather overwrought."

"A bit of help wouldn't go amiss. But I wouldn't want to take you away from your knitting! Heaven forbid!"

"I would help you, of course but I'm just at a really tricky bit and I can't put it down at the moment."

"Why doesn't that surprise me? Well, don't mind me. I'll just carry on setting the table, cooking a meal, washing up and tidying away. I'll be fine. Don't worry about me."

"If you insist. But, leave time for a nap, won't you, dear? Or you'll be biting everyone's head off."

At five to seven, Timothy Bagshaw and his wife of three months, Pandora, pulled up outside his aunt's large Victorian farmhouse. Pandora began to open the door.

"No, don't go in yet, Sweetings. I told you Auntie Alice doesn't like it if one's early."

192

"But it's six fifty-six. Surely she won't mind us being four minutes early?"

"We don't want to antagonise her, do we? It's only another few minutes, Sweetings. Let's just sit here and enjoy the countryside. And remember, if we play our cards right, one day, this view will all be ours."

"Yes, I suppose so, Baggy. I must admit, it would be wonderful to live here. I timed the journey from the railway station in town and it's only fifteen minutes. We could get into London in about two hours in the morning. And at the weekends, we could just relax. Perfect! All we have to do is charm Auntie Alice."

"That may not be as easy as you anticipate."

"I will ooze charm, Baggy darling."

Pandora got out of the car before he could stop her. Oh well, it was only two minutes to seven. Timothy snatched the bottle of wine, box of chocolates and bouquet from the back seat and ran to catch her up. She was struggling with the rusty latch on the wooden gate.

"This will have to go, Baggy. It's falling off its hinges. But the front garden is large enough for an in and out drive. We could have railings and electric gates…"

"Yes, but let's get one thing over at a time." Timothy checked his watch. It was seven o'clock and to his relief, in the distance, church bells began to chime the hour. The grandfather clock inside Aunt Alice's hall bonged as well. He realised his brow was sweating. So much rested on this. More than Pandora knew. He'd just completed a rather large business deal which would make a tidy sum – hopefully. Pandora might have described it as a gamble if she'd known, but then she didn't have much idea of high finance. Owning an art gallery was all well and good but it would be even better if she occasionally sold something.

He paused at the front door, waiting for the grandfather clock to stop bonging.

Timothy pressed the bell and mopped his forehead.

"You must remember, Sweetings, Auntie Alice *is* quite eccentric."

"I've never met anyone I can't handle, Baggy. Just leave her to me. She'll be eating out of my hand before the evening's over. Trust me."

"And don't forget about Auntie Alice's imaginary friend, Margery."

At the tinkle of the doorbell, Alice pressed the intercom button and watched as the screen blinked to life. The black and white, rather grainy image showed two people waiting outside on her doorstep. She didn't recognise the woman, and the man's face was concealed behind an enormous bunch of flowers but she was in no doubt of their identity because their voices blared from the intercom's speaker. The nasal whine of her nephew, Timothy, was quite unmistakeable and anyway, no one else referred to her as 'Auntie Alice'.

She tightly gripped the handle of the knife which she'd been using to hack chunks of bread off a loaf.

Eccentric! He'd just called her *eccentric*! And referred to Margery as *imaginary*! How dare he? But they were still speaking, obviously unaware she could hear them.

"Yes, Baggy, you told me about Marge," the woman said.

"It's Margery, not Marge! For goodness sake, Sweetings, get her name right!"

"Yes, yes, of course. And I'll remember to say hello. The only thing I'm not sure of, is how to know where Margery's supposed to be."

"Well, I usually watch where Auntie Alice is looking

194

when she speaks to her and take my cue from that. You'll get the hang of it. I think Margery normally sits in front of the fire knitting, so after you've said hello, you can more or less forget about her."

"You're talking about Margery as if she's real, Baggy!" Pandora laughed and nudged him, "Should I be worried? Does craziness run in the family?"

"No, Sweetings! Of course not but it makes it easier to handle Auntie Alice if you try to think of Margery as real. Remember, we want her to like us. I mean Auntie Alice – not Margery!"

"Don't worry, Baggy! I know what to do. Shall I ring again? She's taking an awfully long time to come to the door."

Alice glared at the monitor as Timothy checked his watch and the woman's face increased in size on the screen, becoming distorted like a reflection in the back of the bowl of a spoon, as she leaned forward to press the doorbell again.

"D'you think she's forgotten we're coming?" the woman asked frowning at the door.

"I don't know." Timothy checked his watch again and mopped his brow.

"She was getting a bit forgetful the last time I saw her. She forgot to sign the cheque she sent for Christmas and then when I brought it back, she got a bit muddled and signed the wrong name."

The woman groaned, "And to think I turned down the Grosvenor's dinner party so we could spend the evening with an imaginary woman who's a knitaholic and a real woman who's completely nuts. Although," she added, her expression becoming rather calculating, "if she is getting forgetful, that could really work in our favour."

"Hmm, d'you think I should go round the back of the

195

house and look for her? She may have had a fall or something…"

"Good grief, I hope nothing's happened to her. Not 'til we know who she's named in her will. She might leave the lot to the local cats' home."

"No, I'm sure she wouldn't do that, Sweetings. I'm her only nephew. She wouldn't treat me like that.

"Well, Baggy, you did say she was completely crackers. She might do anything."

The woman's face once again became enormous and misshapen, as she leaned towards the doorbell and kept her finger on it.

"Alice!" called Margery from the dining room, "Your guests have arrived!"

Alice would have liked to stay and listen but the persistent tinkling of the doorbell was getting on her nerves. Still clutching the bread knife, she stomped out of the kitchen towards the hall.

"*Forgetful? Nuts? Crackers?* How dare they! And she'll have me eating out of her hand, will she?" Alice muttered as she walked past the dining room door, "We'll see about that!"

"I hope you had a nap, dear," called Margery.

Alice threw open the front door.

"Timothy! How lovely to see you," Alice said, "and this must be your lovely new wife, Pamela."

"I'm Pandora," said Pandora stepping forward, putting out her hand and then thinking better of it as she saw the bread knife.

"Yes, indeed. Pandora. Well, what am I thinking keeping you waiting on the doorstep? Come in, come in."

Timothy and Pandora looked nervously at the knife. Alice smiled inwardly. If she had to put up with entertaining them all evening, she was jolly well going to enjoy herself at their expense. As she led them into the dining room, she knew their eyes were on her, watching to see if she would speak to Margery who was winking from the chair in front of the fire.

"Um, it is just us for dinner?" Timothy asked, his eyes roving the room looking for some sign that Margery was there.

"Well, I asked Margery but…"

"Oh dear, she couldn't come?" Pandora asked with relief.

"Oh no, she's here," said Alice looking towards the door. The young couple turned and Timothy self-consciously raised his hand to greet his aunt's imaginary friend. "But she's working on a tricky piece of knitting and won't join us for dinner," Alice added turning and peering at the chair in front of the fire. Timothy and Pandora swung round, unsure where they should be directing their attention and Timothy held both hands up, hoping that wherever his aunt thought her friend was, he was waving hello.

"You look like you're surrendering, Timothy," Alice said.

"No, no, just waving to dear Margery."

"Oh, how lovely!" said Alice. "See how she's blowing you both kisses!"

Timothy and Pandora sheepishly blew kisses to what seemed to them to be an empty room, spreading them about so that surely some would find the invisible Margery.

"Are you all right, Timothy?" Alice asked as he dabbed his forehead with a handkerchief, "you look a bit hot."

"I'm fine, thank you, Auntie Alice. And may I say, you're looking splendid."

"More soup?" Alice asked.

"No, thank you, that was delicious," said Pandora who had merely agitated it with her spoon and touched it to her

197

lips from time to time. She couldn't stand tomato soup. She was sure the Grosvenors would be serving something rather spectacular as a starter. Something with avocado or hummus.

Alice cleared away the soup bowls and as she left the room, Pandora tried to catch Timothy's gaze but he was studiously ignoring her. He was staring at the chair where they believed Margery was sitting with her knitting. Surely he didn't really believe there was anyone there? But before she could tap his arm and attract his attention, Alice appeared at the dining room door, pushing her trolley, on which was the main course. A gust of wind blew the aroma ahead of the stew and Pandora's stomach lurched with revulsion.

Alice ladled stew onto plates and offered the tinned potatoes and peas to her guests to help themselves.

"So, Timothy, tell me about your wedding," Alice said brightly, "Was I invited?"

"No, Auntie. Pandora and I were married in Barbados, so we only asked our closest fam—"

"One or two people," cut in Pandora who'd foreseen that an only aunt might have considered herself 'close family'. "It was very low key, wasn't it, Baggy?" She kicked him under the table.

"Ow! Oh yes! Very low-key. And hot. And humid. Quite uncomfortable really. Not your sort of thing, I don't suppose, Auntie."

"I'd love to go to Barbados," said Alice, "I've always wanted to travel…"

"Oh, you wouldn't like it, Auntie! Travelling is very expensive. And rather over-rated. it's much nicer being home."

"Yes, perhaps you're right," she said.

There was silence for a few minutes while Timothy and Pandora tried to stab and cut the tinned potatoes which were as hard and slippery as wax balls.

"Mmm, delicious," said Pandora finding what appeared to be a lump of grey meat in the stew. She skewered it with her fork. What sort of meat was it?

"Do you like cats?" Alice asked.

Pandora froze with the fork mid-way to her mouth.

"Umm, I'm not sure," said Pandora returning her fork to the plate and easing the lump off with her knife. Timothy had frozen mid-chew.

"Well, you must know if you like them. Some people seem to prefer cats as pets and others would rather have a dog. I don't like either, as it happens," said Alice.

"Oh, I see," said Pandora, "pets, yes, of course. Well, no, not really, I'm not very keen on animals."

"On the other hand," said Alice, "I don't like to see them hurt. I had a letter this morning from the local cats' home asking for donations. I'm not sure if I should get involved but they do such good work, don't you think?"

"Umm, yes, I'm sure they do, although..." said Pandora poking her husband under the table to kick-start him into giving an argument to dissuade his aunt. Timothy, however, had problems of his own. He'd been chewing a gristly piece of meat and managed to swallow half of it but a long string of slimy connective tissue still joined it to the piece in his mouth. Chew as hard as he might, the two pieces would not be parted. There was nothing for it, he'd simply have to swallow the large piece that was still in his mouth. The hefty lump followed the smaller one down his gullet, his eyes watering and bulging with the effort.

"Yes, indeed," he finally spluttered, mopping his eyes, "but I think most animal homes do very well financially. Lots of people leave money to them in their wills. They can almost wallpaper the walls with bank notes."

"Really? What a waste," said Alice, "I wonder if many people know that. It's such a worry wondering what one should do with one's money when one's gone."

"Yes, indeed, Auntie. Well, as you know, I work for an investment company and I'd be glad to advise you. No charge, of course!"

"That would be very useful, Timothy. What sort of things do you think you might recommend?"

"Oh, property. Always property. You can't go wrong with bricks and mortar."

"So, do you suggest I buy another property?"

Timothy's eyes lit up, "That's a really good idea, Auntie."

"But I couldn't live in two properties, what would I do with the other one?"

"Rent it out." Timothy nudged Pandora under the table and gave her a glimmer of a smile. This was going better than they'd anticipated.

"Hmm, that's not a bad idea, Timothy. But I don't know much about buying and renting. Is it hard? How do you find people who want to rent? Suppose they turn out to be totally unsuitable?"

"Well, that is a risk, of course but I'm sure I could find you some tenants you could trust."

"It just so happens Baggy and I are looking for a new place to live," said Pandora. "You'd be able to trust us. We'd look after everything as if it was ours, wouldn't we Baggy, darling?"

"Oh, yes indeed."

Pandora and Timothy grinned at each other in delight.

Alice saw their triumphant smiles but chose to ignore them. Instead, she turned towards the chair in front of the fire and said loudly, "I don't think they heard you, Margery dear, I'll ask them."

To the young couple, she said, "Margery would like to know where you suggest buying."

"This would be a perfect location," said Timothy. "Lots of lovely countryside but close enough to commute to London."

Alice cocked her head as if listening to Margery, her face turned towards the chair near the fire.

Pandora and Timothy looked from Alice to the chair and then back again.

"Yes, dear," said Alice finally, "I think that's a wonderful idea."

"Umm, what's that, Auntie?" Timothy asked.

"Margery says it's a marvellous idea to buy a house…"

Timothy beamed and poked Pandora under the table with his foot in a victory prod.

"She's obviously a woman with a lot of financial know-how," he said pompously.

"And," added Alice, "she said if I buy a house, she'd be happy to rent it. What a perfect solution! How soon can we start?"

"On the other hand," said Pandora, "buying and renting property can be very stressful…" she kicked Timothy under the table.

"But I thought you said you can't go wrong with bricks and mortar, Timothy?"

"Well, yes but it doesn't suit everyone."

"How about art?" said Pandora, "Some people like to invest in pieces of art, don't they, Baggy?"

He nodded vigorously, struggling with his final mouthful of stew.

"Hmm, well you've both given me a lot to think about. It's so refreshing to have impartial advice. Excuse me while I go and get dessert."

"Oh, I couldn't eat another thing," said Pandora, pushing her plate towards Alice. It still seemed to be as full as it had been at the beginning of the main course.

"Nonsense!" said Alice, "Everyone loves dessert. I'll be right back. Come on Margery, come and help me."

Alice pushed the trolley out of the dining room, closed the door and put her ear to it.

"You really are very naughty, Alice," whispered Margery, "you're running rings round those poor innocents."

"Serve them right. Shhh! I want to hear what they've got to say."

"Are you sure Margery's gone?" Timothy said.

"Baggy! Don't be so ridiculous! She's *imaginary!*"

"I know, I know, this place just gets under my skin!"

"That's ridiculous! It's just a house. And a rather large, desirable house at that. It's your nutty aunt who's unnerving you."

There was silence for a few seconds.

"You know, Baggy, if she's so out of touch with reality, perhaps she'd be better off in a home… We could manage her affairs. She needs someone to care for her. I mean, just look at this tablecloth, it's full of holes. Who in their right mind would set a table like this? Yes, she'd be better off being looked after."

"Auntie Alice'd never go into a home. And what about Margery?"

"Baggy! Margery is imaginary!"

"Yes, yes, of course! But how would we persuade Auntie to go?"

"The woman is completely crackers. As nutty as a fruitcake. She needs to be looked after. It would be a kindness."

"Yes, you might be right, Sweetings. It would be a kindness. And I'm sure Margery could move in with her."

Alice hurried into the kitchen and replaced the plates with dessert bowls. She then noisily returned to the dining room.

"So sorry to have left you for so long," she said, "I'm

afraid I couldn't find the tinned custard, so I had to use a packet."

"No custard for me, thank you," said Pandora as Alice poured sauce over her pudding.

"You can't possibly eat sponge pudding without," said Alice and placed it in front of her.

Pandora reluctantly dipped her spoon into the bowl and raised it to her lips. She frowned as the aroma reached her olfactory receptors.

"Is the custard all right, Auntie?" Timothy asked through a half-eaten mouthful, "It's got a very strange flavour."

"You weren't listening, dear," said Alice. "I told you I couldn't find the tinned custard."

"This doesn't taste like custard from a packet, Auntie."

"No, dear, it's cheese sauce. I didn't have any packets of custard either."

"Mmm, very nice, and how unusual. Pudding and cheese board all in one," said Pandora placing her spoon in the bowl and dabbing the corners of her mouth delicately with her napkin.

"Now," said Alice brightly, "How has married life been?"

"Oh, wonderful, Auntie, although it's hard for young people to keep their heads above water in the current financial climate, you know," said Timothy.

"Yes," said Pandora, "it's been a bit of a struggle, really."

"Oh dear," said Alice. "Well I should be able to help you out a bit. And since I wasn't invited to your wedding, I didn't send you a present, so I really must make it up to you."

Timothy and Pandora kicked each other under the table and beamed delightedly.

"Well, Auntie, that's really kind."

"What did you have in mind?" asked Pandora.

"I'm not sure…"

"I still have my wedding present list, if that would help," suggested Pandora.

"No, I'm sure I'll think of something suitable. It should be a gift that will always remind you of me."

"They're going to be very disappointed if you don't send them anything," said Margery once Timothy and Pandora had gone.

"I *am* going to send them a gift. I'm a woman of my word."

"You are?"

"Of course. And what's more, I've decided I'm going to make Timothy my beneficiary. I'll get a new will drawn up."

"Really?"

"Yes, of course. It was you who pointed out he's my only nephew."

"I know but their attempts to get you to sign everything over to them were so obvious – even I spotted them and I don't exist," said Margery. "Surely you're not going to let them get away with it. Good grief, they were talking about putting you in a home! Where's your self-respect?"

"Oh, don't you worry, I'm going to have the last laugh."

"Really?"

"Absolutely."

Two days later, Alice returned from town looking very pleased with herself.

"Margery? Where are you?"

"By the fire."

"Well, go and get packed. We're going on a cruise to

the Caribbean. I've booked us one of the most expensive suites. We leave tomorrow."

"Really?"

"Yes, we're going to kick our knees up in Barbados!"

"Isn't it *heels*?"

"Isn't what *heels*?"

"You kick your heels up, not your knees."

"Well, then we'll do a knees-up. And we're going to do it with no expense spared in Barbados and all around the Caribbean!"

"Won't that be dreadfully expensive?"

"Dreadfully. I might have to sell the house and buy something much smaller. In fact, I think we ought to spend the next few years travelling the world – until I drop my clogs or the money runs out – whichever happens first."

"I like your thinking, Alice."

Margery finished the row, rammed the ball of wool over the end of the needles and put the knitting in her bag, "Right, I'm packed."

"And don't worry about Timothy and Pandora. I've sent them a gift as I promised. Something to remind them of me," said Alice.

A very large box arrived at the Bagshaw's house the following day, addressed to Timothy and Pamela Bagshaw.

"It's from Auntie Alice," said Timothy, slicing open the top and pulling out the letter which sat on top of the polystyrene packing chips.

"Sweetings! Look at this! Auntie Alice is going to make me her sole beneficiary! She's had a new will drawn up! You're a marvel! You said you'd have her eating out of your hand the other evening. That disgusting meal was worth every minute. Although I must admit, things didn't seem to be going very well at the time. But all's well that ends well."

Pandora squealed with delight. "What's in the box, Baggy?" she asked, excitedly, scooping out handfuls of polystyrene shapes.

"Oh!" she said with disappointment as she held up a fruitcake, "Is it some kind of food hamper?"

Timothy delved into the box and brought out several packets of mixed, salted nuts.

"Wait!" said Timothy, "There's another box in here." He pulled it out and sliced it open. They peered inside.

"Crackers for cheese," Timothy read on the side of one of the packets. He looked at Pandora with incomprehension "Twenty-four packets of crackers," he said.

"Fruitcake… nuts… crackers…" whispered Pandora, her eyes wide with alarm, "That's how I described your aunt, the other evening when we went to her house. She said she'd send us something to remind us of her."

"But… but Auntie wasn't there. How did she know, Sweetings? It was only you, me and…" Timothy gasped, "You don't think Margery crept back into the dining room when we weren't looking…?"

"No! That's simply ridiculous, Baggy! It couldn't possibly have been Margery! She's imaginary!" said Pandora. "Isn't she?"

About the author
Dawn's third and latest book is *Extraordinary*, an anthology published by Bridge House Publishing. She has stories published in other anthologies, including horror and speculative fiction, as well as romances in women's magazines. Dawn has written a play to commemorate World War One, which has been performed in England, Germany and France.

www.dawnknox.com

Up in Smoke

Paula R C Readman

"I've always loved this time of year, especially November. As a child it always seemed magical to me," James Peterson said to the driver of the van he'd hired for the day.

"Right," the driver said rolling his eyes with an air of disinterest as he checked his mirrors. Then he glanced over at James, and with a nod let out a long sigh. "Please could you belt up, Sir."

"What! Oh sorry, yes, of course," James snapped the belt together with a satisfying clunk.

The driver pacified, gave a sharp nod, readjusted his rear view mirror, and then gave a final check to the road behind before joining the early morning traffic.

James leant back in his seat, hoping for a comfortable ride. He didn't want to think about the task ahead, when he had plenty of other things that needed doing. He stared out of the window, enjoying the sight of people rushing about in the busy cityscape. He knew the first part of the journey would be slow. Too many traffic lights and dawdling cyclists caught up in the morning rush hour, but at least it gave him the chance to enjoy the architecture when under normal circumstances it flashed past.

As the cityscape faded making way for a more rural setting, he gave a snort, soon losing interest in his surroundings.

In the silence of the van's cab, he glanced over at the driver who seemed lost in his own thoughts.

James normally used to the busyness of an office was unable to cope with the silence, and felt the need to shatter the peace.

207

"It's my birthday today," James stated.

"Oh, happy birthday, Sir" the driver replied as he swung the van into the fast lane to overtake a slow moving lorry.

"Thanks," James said brightly, not wanting anything to dampen his happiness. "Well, my official birthday is in eleven days' time, but my father and I always celebrated ours together."

"Really, how nice for you." The driver manoeuvred back into the middle lane again.

"As a kid, I always thought so. We used to have lots of fireworks and the all-important bonfire."

The driver glanced at him. "I suppose being bonfire night it's only natural. Though living in a city, I can't see it was legal, with pollution regulations, Mr Peterson."

"No, Err… Sorry, what's your name?"

"Colin." The driver checked his rear view mirror.

"Well, Colin, I grew up in the countryside. That's where we're heading now. Dad let me help him build the bonfire. "Stack it high, lad," he used to say, and "Stand well back," when it came time to light it. Far better than candles on a cake when the flames caught, I always thought. You see, I was lucky enough to live on the edge of a forest, so I could have a bonfire on my birthday every year."

The driver let out a sigh. "Wow, how lovely. Growing up next to a forest is something special. What did your father do for a…?"

James interrupted, "He was a forester. What he doesn't know about trees isn't worth knowing."

"That's a dying art, Mr Peterson. Guess he learnt his trade the old fashioned way by serving an apprenticeship."

James stared out of the window, and studied the tree-lined motorway. "I don't know," he said, "I never thought to ask him."

Colin glanced over at Mr Peterson. "Didn't you think about learning your father's craft?"

James snorted again. "Me follow in my old man's footsteps? No way."

Colin checked his side mirror before moving into the fast lane. "Cor, I would've loved it. Learning an old craft like that, instead of being stuck at the wheel all day. Rushing from one point to another isn't a great way to make a living. I hardly see my family. My kids would love it, growing up next to a wood, especially our Betty, surrounded by nature every day. Not a bad job, I would say."

"Colin, it's all about the money, mate. Give me the city every time. I'm a bright lights and endless noise sort of guy. It was okay, while I was growing up, having your very own wild wood on your doorstep, but seeing my old man wet through after shifting tons of wood day after day. Not for me."

"Well, Mr Peterson, I'm the third generation to have grown up on the same housing estate. As a kid, I dreamt of having a garden as we lived in a flat on the seventh floor. I would've gladly swapped places with you and enjoyed seeing the seasons changing. All we had in the way of wild life were pigeons, burnt-out cars, and endless streams of windswept rubbish. The only way we knew the season had changed was because the playing field, muddy in winter and full of gulls, had become sun baked in the summer."

"I guess your parents read you the same book as mine. The wild wood, ha, ha. Every kid's dream. I too went hunting for Mr Badger after Dad read that book aloud to me at bedtime. God, for the life of me I can't remember the name of it? Full of old stoats and weasels... oh damn! Funny, how things come back to you."

209

"The Wind in the Willows," Colin said, changing lanes again.

"Are you sure? I thought it was Tales from the Riverbank?"

"No, that's a television programme with Johnny Morris's voice-over hamster."

"Oh."

"So does your father still...?"

"Still in the same old cottage," James cut in. "Never wanted to move. It's not his, it came with the job."

"Bet it's a picturesque place?" Colin gave a heavy sigh as the traffic began to slow.

"Well, I suppose you could call it that. Not my sort of thing, or taste. A small, squat building with flint walls, a high chimney, and acres of garden surrounded by the wood. I'm what you might call a lover of contemporary style. I'm one for moving with the times and live in a warehouse conversion that I got at a good price. They say you can tell a lot about someone by where they live..."

"Myself, Mr Peterson, I like a place with a bit of history."

"There's history and then there's ancient," James said taking the conversation back. "My grandparents had the cottage before my parents. Both, my father and I were born there."

"Sort of a family tree then?" Colin said with a chuckle.

"Oh yes, family tree... very funny," James snapped, "but what you don't appreciate is your family might not enjoy growing up in some rotten old cottage. I suppose there wasn't the same sort of choice in available accommodation when my father took it over."

Colin gave a sideward glance at the well-dressed, over-fed city gent, and shook his head slowly.

"Oh god, now what?" James moaned as the traffic

ground to a halt. After a moment of silence, he continued, "Now you come to mention it, I think my father had to move back home to look after my grandparents. Well, that's what they did in those days, didn't they?"

Colin shrugged after checking his mirror and said, "Yes, my mother looked after my father's parents. They lived in the flat next door which made it much easier for her to keep an eye on them. My sister and I enjoyed spending time with them after school as our parents worked. Back then, there was a real sense of community unlike these days. Too much crime has spoiled it."

"Crime... not something, we get where I live," James said proudly. "Anyway, my wife and I don't have time in our busy schedule to look after my father."

"Oh, so you're not having him to live with you then?"

"No way! Knowing my father as I do, Colin, he'll be happier with a space of his own. I've found the ideal home for him. Well, it's more an apartment in a home for the retired. There's plenty to amuse him, daytrips to the seaside, and bingo too. Old people like that sort of thing, don't they?"

"I take it you've chatted to him about it."

"Why should I talk to him about it? He knows I'm only doing what's best for him. He can't live by himself forever. Not only that, he'll have people around him of his own age..."

"If you haven't talked it over with him, how do you know?"

"Look, no offence, Colin, but I've hired you to drive, not to tell me what's best for my father. Anyway, I've made sure he has everything he needs, or wants at the home. He can look at trees all day. I've been told that there's a park nearby..."

"Nope, you're right, none of my business, Mr Peterson.

How much further before we turn off?"

"Not much further now."

"That's good," Colin muttered, pleased at the thought of not spending much longer in the company of such a man.

"Sorry, what did you say?"

"The foliage looks lovely."

"Yes, I suppose, it does, but it makes a hell of a mess. That's how I earnt my pocket money, raking up leaves for Dad. I don't miss it one bit. Anyway, Dad will be pleased to see me. I know it's been a while since my last visit. I called him the other night, just to let him know I would be there to help him pack."

"What you just phoned your father out of the blue, and told him to pack his things?"

"Yes, it took some persuading, but he saw sense in the end. Once I explained how lucky he was to be moving into such a brilliant home at such short notice."

"You mean to say you haven't shown him where he'll be living."

"Not that it's any of your business, but a friend of mine said it came highly recommended, and she should know because they got her old mother into the place."

"But surely you've made sure that the home is ideal."

"Look, what you don't understand is I've a busy schedule, and need to be in New York by the weekend."

"Aren't you being a bit hard on him, doing it all at such short notice?"

"Me, being a bit hard on him! Father will understand. As a child, he was always telling me to grow up, and get on with my life. So I have, haven't I?"

"Look, I know I don't know your father, but…"

James interrupted, "Okay so I might seem a bit heartless to you, but there comes a point in all our lives when we can no longer look after ourselves."

"Oh, sorry, Mr Peterson, if your father is incapable of looking after himself, then I've misjudged you. Obviously if your father is having problems then, of course, you're doing the right thing for his own safety."

"That's life, isn't it?" James said with a grin. "It gets to us all in the end. I cannot believe how lucky I've been this week, with you having this van free at short notice, so I could do it all in one go."

"Maybe you should've found time in your busy schedule to have gone over a couple of weeks earlier, you know, just to help him sort things out."

"Father doesn't have much to sort out. I helped him sort everything out after Mum passed away. Well, I didn't see much point in keeping everything that wasn't worth much."

"Okay, right. As you said, 'money is everything', but what about the sentimental value."

"Sentimental value, what rot! You only have to watch Antiques Road Show to see sentimental value go out the window when people hear how much their precious items are worth in a monetary sense. Kuching! And the sentimentality disappears in a puff of banknotes."

"So you do get some spare time in your busy schedule then?"

"Sorry," James said puzzled for a moment. "Oh yes, I never miss Antiques Road Show. One can always learn a lot from it. Did you see it the other weekend?"

"No. Don't really have much time at the weekend what with…"

"Well, it's a good job I did. One of their experts was rabbiting on about some old bits of furniture designed by a guy called Chippendale being worth about £150,000 each. I couldn't believe it, and there was me thinking that the Chippendales were a bunch of male strippers."

Colin chuckled, and turned off the motorway.

213

"You may laugh, but just remember what they say about, he who laughs last laughs the longest. Anyway, my old Dad has some bits of furniture made by Mr Chippendale. No word of a lie, he's sitting on a small fortune."

"That's good so he'll be comfortably off in the home."

"What? No, he won't need it. That's the beauty of the place, I've chosen for him. The running costs are low. Okay, so it's just a tiny flat, but at least it has everything he needs. Well, as for money, he has his pension." James suddenly pointed at the road ahead, "Turn there."

Colin turned into a narrow lane.

"We're nearly there now. It's not much further. Just round the next bend. You can see the chimney top from here. That's odd, I can see smoke. Don't tell me, he's lit a fire? I hope Dad isn't going to make this difficult for me."

"Maybe he's just been raking up the leaves, wanting everything tidy before he goes."

"Yeah, you could be right, which is just the reason why he'll be better off in the home, nothing for him to worry about anymore. No leaves to rake and central heating. It does look like bonfire smoke, doesn't it? Why has he made a bonfire today of all days?"

"I thought you said it's a family tradition, or have you forgotten about gunpowder, treason, and plot?"

"Oh no his birthday… Yes, I forgot… Treason? Oh, very funny, oh, I see what you mean November 5th, the gunpowder plot. You're a joke a minute, aren't you? Ha, ha"

"Wow, what an amazing place! When you said a shack of a cottage, I didn't imagine something like this. Built in the 1600's I would guess."

"That's right. So you're a history buff too then, Colin. If you go through those gates on your left, and park it over there," James said, pointing to a parking space beneath a tree.

"Does your father have someone to look after the garden then?"

"No, it's all his work." James said with a frown.

"But you said… He must be pretty fit for his age."

"Oh yes he's always been active. Just wish I took after him on that score, but sitting at a desk all day."

The driver rolled his eyes.

"I'll have you know, I have a gym membership, but with my busy…"

"Yes, I know your schedule. What do you do then, Mister High Flyer, something big in the city, no doubt?"

"Yes, you could put it that way. I'm an accountant. I like to balance the books. Now I wonder what Dad's burning. He must be round the back, if you would like to follow me."

Colin watched as James hauled his bulk out of the van and shuffled across to the side gate.

"Come this way. Dad'll be in the garden."

To Colin's surprise, he found himself standing in a beautiful well-kept garden full of neat flowering borders, and trimmed leaf-free lawns.

"Hello Dad. Where are you?" James called into the cottage on hearing no answer he turned to the hired-help. "Sorry mate, if you wait here. I'll not be long." He stepped into the neat kitchen. "Hang on; it looks like he's already packed everything. There's just some odd bags and a couple of boxes, but where's the furniture?"

As James disappeared from view, Colin watched a tall, elegant man with a head of thick white hair come strolling up a flagstone path, carrying a rake over his shoulder.

"Hello, can I help you, lad?" The man said.

"Err, Mister Peterson?" Colin said.

"Yes, I am. And you are?"

"I'm Colin, the hired help. Your son's indoors. Oh, and by the way, happy birthday, Sir."

"Thank you, Colin. Please call me Bill."

"Your garden is amazing, and I see you grow your own vegetables too."

"My pride and joy, especially when my Annie was alive. You can't beat home-grown vegetables."

"Wow, I'd love to give my kids a chance to grow vegetables and the freedom to run around in a place like this."

"Really?"

"Yes, Sir. Your son was telling me about his childhood, very different to mine. I'm a city guy with the countryside in my heart. We've tried to grow things in pots but to have the space like this…"

"Oh, my son isn't happy unless it comes from Harrods. The tenancy on this place is coming up soon. If you're interested I could put in a word for you."

"Oh wow, I would love to live here. I'm self-employed, so I could soon find work locally."

"If you have a business card, I could let you know."

"Why, thank you Mr Peterson, that's very kind of you." Colin handed over his card.

"My pleasure, Colin. Now where's that son of mine."

Mr Peterson reached the door, just as James stepped out into the fading afternoon sunlight, his cheeks red.

Breathing heavily, he held onto the door frame. "Oh, there you are Dad. I don't know how you managed those stairs at your age?"

"They don't bother me, Son. Did you have a good look about?"

216

"Err, yes. I see you have a bonfire on the go. Isn't it a bit late in the afternoon to start one?"

"I haven't just started. It's been on the go all day, burning some of the leaves, and rubbish. I didn't see the point of taking it with me, if I'm making a fresh start in my old age."

"Oh, I see, you're just finishing up?"

"Are you all right, James? You're looking a bit pale. Oh, I didn't get my birthday card, this morning."

"Sorry, had a lot on my mind with work. Anyway, are you ready to go?

"You shouldn't have wasted your money on such a big van, Son."

"Of course the van isn't too big, Dad. Where's the furniture?"

"Son, all I have is what's in the…"

James didn't wait for his father to finish he hurried as fast as his bulk would allow along the path towards the bonfire.

Mr Peterson turned to the hired-help, "What on earth has got into him?"

"He thinks you've burnt the furniture, Sir."

"Does he now? Well, I'm not one for the telly, but I happened to see *Antiques Roadshow* the other day and was shocked to see my furniture on there. I called in a dealer, and got a good price. Just between you and me, Colin, I've always dreamt about visiting the forests of the world, from Canada to the rainforests of Malaysia. I don't know how long I'll be away for, but I won't need so much. So if you're happy about taking on the job of looking after this place for an indefinite amount of time, I'll know it'll be in good hands."

"You've bought this place?"

"Yes, years ago." Bill laughed. "No doubt my son will

have a moan about it, but I've always loved it."

"He doesn't know?" Colin laughed too.

"Nope, I'd like to keep it that way too. I thought I'd take up my son's offer of clearing the house because it was cheaper than the local companies. In the end with the sale of the furniture I didn't need a van after all."

"Couldn't you have let him know?"

"My busy schedule didn't allow for it. Anyway, I need him to look after a few bits until I come home, whenever that may be. And it's the only way I could've got him to come and see me."

"Good for you, Sir."

"Thank you, Colin. Now don't you worry about your tenancy agreement, I'll have it all drawn up properly before I go." Mister Peterson gave a wink, and put his finger to his lip. "Shh, here comes that son of mine. Don't say anything; he'll have whatever's left when I've gone, if any."

"Dad, I can't believe you burnt all Mum's lovely furniture."

"Sorry Son, I didn't realise you were so attached to it. When I asked you about the furniture not long after Mum died you told me you didn't want that old junk in your flat."

"But Mum loved it."

On seeing the devastation on the city-flyer face, Colin bent to stifle a laugh as he picked up a couple of bags and headed towards the van.

James managed to pick up a couple of small boxes and followed him. As he passed the boxes to the hired-help, he said, "I can't believe what my father has just done. A small fortune has gone up in smoke."

As Colin took the boxes, he gave a slight nod. "Well, you did say, he who laughs last laughs the longest, Mister Peterson."

About the author

Paula R. C. Readman lives in Essex. In 2010, her first success was with English Heritage who selected her story for *Whitby Abbey – Pure Inspiration*. Since then she's had several other short stories published and won two writing competitions. Paula was one of 16 winners in the Waterloo Festival Writing Competition 2018.

Find out more about Paula and her writing on her Amazon Author page or on her blog:
http://paulareadman1.wordpress.com

Very Little Helps

Clare Weze

Normally, the café is too busy to overhear customers' conversations, but today is deathly quiet. There's a craft festival in St John Street. His workmates have been sent there to man a pop-up café and most of his regular customers have defected too, so Markus can hear every word the only two punters in the place utter. Every. Sodding. Word. They're in their sixties – or maybe their seventies, it's hard to tell – and they're ladies dressed to lunch, even though it's late in the day. A talker and a listener. The talker, who's white, is well curled into the chat, like such types always are, and the listener – a black woman – is taking it like it's medicine.

The words roll over him at first, but then something in the monotony of her tone makes him tune in. Just to see what could be that dry. Dry, yet pulsing. Pressing. And Jesus. It's all about her oil-fired central heating boiler. The listening one can't steer the conversation. She has a feeble try every so often, but *BOILER. BOILER MAN. SERVICE AGREEMENT. BOILER* just steamrolls her.

Markus wipes the counter down in rough, zig-zagging sweeps and wonders why the boring one wants an audience when a wall would do. He shoves the cloth onwards to the sink sloppily, thinking of his colleagues, Doog and Mali, who will be well underway by now. They were chosen to run the pop-up café at the festival because they out-hipster him. Jacob, the manager, has left Markus in charge – yet again – because he says he's solid and dependable. It wasn't his ambition to be dependable. Jacob says something about dependable Hungarians, but that's bullshit, because Markus's British Hungarian mum lost touch with the

220

Hungarian side of the family, so he knows embarrassingly little about Hungary. He just pictures the Danube and all the lights in Budapest, like everyone else.

He looks across at the ladies again. The rabbiter tilts her head and maintains eye contact with the poor listener, forcing her to pretend to be engaging in the whole crap topic. The strain must be mammoth. She's nodding, at intervals. *BOILER. BOILER MAN. New boiler servicing agreement. Pig of a thing to manage. BOILER. Not as if he's the only one in Cardiff. So I told him he'd meet himself coming back at those rates.*

The listening one crowbars two words in, but they're just pummelled back by the boiler talk. Markus surreptitiously searches her face to see if she's ready to die of the conversation, but if anything, she just looks a bit sad. There's surely real danger of their combined life-force being sucked into that rolling, groaning boiler lecture, and there they are, sitting at the window table with a view of the lake that finally fully dried up only last week, leaving all the fish aground. Why not talk about that?

It's always weird here without the others. Without the crack. This morning, Jacob told him to smile at customers a little more often – the trace of Scottish in his accent skittering over the emphasis on 'little more', which he mimed with finger and thumb in his posh, focused, cleverer-than-the-business-he's-in way. This humiliated Markus, on top of the joint humiliation he's felt since Jacob revealed that one of them is stealing from the till. They aren't exactly all equally blamed, but at the same time, there's a tar-brush, and until the culprit's caught – which they won't be now they know Jacob's onto them – that little smear of tar will keep staining, and whenever Jacob mentions 'reclaimed timber' and 'growing the business' and 'fresh challenges', it'll be there.

221

Maybe this isn't really what he should be doing at this point in his life.

The rabbiter's spewing drivel about some kind of freaking blender now. "So I took it back to the shop. They swapped it for me, but... *drivel, drivel, drivel*" Markus tunes out, but for some reason, the line, "You can grate parmesan with this one," reels him back in.

"And Alex is keeping track of my favourite cheeses on a spreadsheet," the rabbiter continues, examining one of her many-ringed fingers.

"Alex?" asks the listener.

"The chap from Greens."

Then it's back to the boiler.

Neither of them has given him so much as a glance, so he's free to monitor them discreetly. Can the rabbiter not see that the listener's eyes have deadened? Awful thing for one person to do to another.

He hates it when the café is godforsaken like this. Time and boredom melt into one long mess. There are half a dozen tidying tasks he could be doing, but he's not much into cleaning. And why should he knock himself out with that shite? It *could* have been rammed in here – Jacob wasn't to know. They could easily have left him in the lurch and running round like a blue-arsed fly. So fuck them anyway.

BOILER. BOILER MAN. SERVICE AGREEMENT. BOILER.

Grim. And she isn't going to stop. The listener nods, her mouth a straight line, hands smoothing an area of serviette over and over. There's a funny sort of patience to the way she listens. Markus doesn't know how she has any, listening to all this junk. Not really that wrinkly, either of them, but the rabbiter is red around the eyes. Probably all that talking. Thinish, she is, with short grey hair in wisps around her ears and neck. Tweedy jacket and dark blue silky blouse. Lots of jewellery. Looks like she'd never dream of smiling. The listener's plumper, in smart jeans and bright jade top, and has a serious, professional air that somehow matches the cortado she sips. Rabbiter has a latte, which Markus has yet to catch her drinking.

BOILER.BOILER MAN.BOILER… This woman thinks she's being sociable. She thinks she's having a nice coffee and a chat. She's not. She's taken a hostage. And something in her tone annoys him. Somehow, it reminds him of all the opportunities not exactly missed, more unseen. In disguise. The tone of it is linking directly to a horrible memory, something that happened back at school, perhaps last year? Something he can't quite remember and doesn't really want to. The listener asks where Rabbiter got her blouse in a thinly veiled attempt to deflect her. It works, but only up to a point, because now she's launched on a diatribe about a department store, with special, excruciating emphasis on words connected to certain makes. *Jaeger. Poggenpohl. Cartier. Lacroix.*

"Did you hear about the fish across the way there, and what happened to them?' the listener asks. 'You know, when all the water went?"

"No."

"They were left stranded, flapping. Lots of them, there were. Dying."

Rabbiter raises her eyebrows and makes a noise at the back of her throat. More choking than clearing. Then she continues: *BOILER.BOILER MAN.BOILER…*

There's beauty out there, and life and death and suffering, yet she focuses on her boiler. Markus runs hot water through the syrup dispenser they call the gloop tap. You never know how it will come out. Gloop today. Slop yesterday. *BOILER.BOILER MAN.BOILER…* When I'm old, I'll have a rule, he thinks: *be interesting, or shut the fuck up.* His thoughts race on a few months, double back, then circle angrily as the running water billows steam high, a hint of bleach in it, like the teabags here always have. Maybe he really should get away from this failed mock-hipster place. Maybe he doesn't have the credentials to make it in the happening places, though. Not enough facial hair. Doog and Mali are both students, but pretend to be bored by their subjects, as if they're above it all. Maybe he should up his plans to save hard and visit Hungary. Really squirrel it. Cut stuff out. But there's never enough spare. And now he realises why this mood is coming off him with this pair: it's the grandmother vibe. Both his grandmothers are lost to him, and none of it was necessary.

BOILER.BOILER MAN.BOILER... He means to travel more, at some point. Soon. That's the idea of working this sort of instant job. City to city, country to country, he's going to go. Definitely. Maybe jack this in September and go to France. *BOILER.BOILER MAN.BOILER...*

The listener catches his eye and Markus's reflex smile kicks in. He wipes his hands on his apron and shifts the music on the sound system round to 'Year of the Cat'. It might suit these customers; he knows it from his mum playing it to death when he was young. *BOILER.BOILER MAN.BOILER...*

Mum. He can do without her in his head again. *BOILER.BOILER MAN.BOILER...* He wishes, for the millionth time, that she hadn't moved them up from London. Something happened to her down there, he suspects, because she's never looked back. And that's not natural. What's wrong with London, for her? He's asked, but she isn't straight with him, just goes on about something or other, boring stuff, jobs, annoying things his

224

grandparents did that aren't really things. And if they hadn't moved to Cardiff, when he was too small to know any different – before Carl was even born – if they hadn't moved, he'd be there now. A Londoner. He'd kept his London accent for a while. Even now, he and Carl speak differently. You can tell they come from different places. It's in the *no, go, show* vowels. And less so in the *gate, wait, late* ones. You can tell Carl's a native Welshman, with a Welsh father. Markus hasn't actually got a drop of Welsh blood in him. He doesn't fully belong here. Not really. And his own dad was a northerner.

There are dismal and dying fruit salads on the display shelf. He should clear those. Instead, he smudges some dried coffee grinds until they crunch like footsteps through snow. Turning things into something else – that's what he should be doing. *BOILER. BOILER MAN. BOILER…*

BOILER. BOILER MAN. BOILER…

BOILER. BOILER MAN. BOILER…

BOILER. BOILER MAN. BOILER…

BOILER. BOILER MAN. BOILER… And now, in a mind-blowingly surreal way, Markus starts to enjoy it, this mad rant. It *is* surreal, if you spin it to yourself that way. And he can see how it could be spun later, when he's with his mates – it really is that extreme. He smiles. Wants to laugh.

As he crouches to stack plates beneath the counter, Markus grins. Almost closing time. Almost time for the island of peace he only gets when on lock-up duty, like today, and can pretend he lives on a lakeside retreat. Noise at work when the café's busy. Noise at home from the main road. Peace here, for a short while.

"There's a lot to be learned from things that aren't working and things that need fixing." The listener says this, and Markus stops what he's doing. He bobs up again and taps the words into his phone. It's given him an idea; it could almost be a road-map for jobs and other life paths.

Then the listener asks, "What did John prefer to do about having the boiler serviced?"

Everything goes quiet. The silence is tightly drawn throughout the room; empty chairs seem to wait in it.

"He used to get Bill Bateson Engineers. But Bill retired around the same time John went downhill..." Rabbiter's voice quivers, then fades out like something that has run down to the end of its range after having been wound for a very long time.

Part of Markus's brain seems to do a double-take. Not his eyes; they don't move. The shock is right inside his head. A corner-of-the-eye revelation. If he'd been so much as running the tap, he'd have missed it. Definitely. Imagine: to have missed the total point of that entire latte saga.

The listener's expression looks lighter, somehow, and she takes a deep breath. "It's something I realised only quite recently," she says, "but actually, our household possessions can be quite artistic and meaningful. Life-affirming. Precious collections. And when we look after them in our activities of daily comfort – that's what I call housework – we soothe ourselves."

Rabbiter's been staring into her coffee cup throughout this speech, and now she nods and lifts her red eyes to meet the listener's.

The listener continues, "It's taken me a long time to reach this conclusion."

Nobody's speaking. He doesn't look at them anymore, but has an instinct that somebody on the table is crying. He'll give it a few minutes, then he'll clear and ask if they'd like anything else.

About the author

Clare Weze writes both for adults and children. She won a Northern Writers' Award for her forthcoming short-story collection, and her work has been placed second, third and shortlisted in several literary prizes. Her short fiction can be found in anthologies by Bridge House Publishing, Curiosity Quills, the Bath Flash Fiction Award and Wonderbox Publishing, and she has had a flash fiction story shortlisted for the Bridport literary festival. Her writing has also appeared online in *The Conglomerate* journal and *Reflex Fiction*, and accompanies the CD of *Clinch Mountain* by musician Fionn Kay-Lavelle. Clare now has an agent.

clareweze.com
@ClareWeze

Years of Eclipse

L F Roth

Sanderson inserts the key. His aim is right, in spite of the dim light. He turns it, expecting the usual barely audible clicking sound as the catch is released, but there is none. Puzzled, he tries the handle. The door opens. Has someone broken in? Don't panic, he orders himself, as his heart beats faster. One slow step at a time he advances into the hall, leaving the door gaping behind him. "Hello," he calls. The silence builds. Advancing, he inspects the bedroom, but everything is as it should be: the bed unmade, his pyjamas spread-eagled across the solitary pillow. Getting rid of its companion had been a good move – his back had improved overnight. As his gaze returns to the hall, he hears the toilet flush and stops in his tracks. The bathroom door swings open. A hand appears, followed by the head and shoulders of what proves to be a squat figure dressed in an overall and wearing a heavy tool belt. If he is a burglar, he must be a professional.

"Sorry about that," says the intruder. "Caught short."

No professional, evidently, but curiously at home. Sanderson remains uneasy: the face wears no name. Is he an electrician come to fix the light in the stairs? Caught short, he may have rung the nearest bell and, after a brief delay, produced his master key. Sanderson probes him.

"You are…?"

"The plumber. Pete Dexter."

There is a wrench among his tools.

"Someone phoned in about a dripping tap."

"They did?" He'd meant to report it, but had he done so? Occasionally, he will write himself a note as a reminder, but notes tend to get lost or else become illegible. His

228

neighbour may have sworn over the dripping late at night when sounds magnify. She wouldn't rest till she got hold of somebody. "You'll have to put in a new…" He breaks off. Having intended to test the man, he himself is on trial. He stares into the distance, but the word he is groping for isn't there. "A whatchamacallit. Like a discus. With a hole."

Dexter, if that is his name, nods. "A washer. The washbasin, is it?"

Sanderson accepts his credentials. "The bath. And the shower. Sometimes there is a drip from both. I don't use the shower much. It doesn't feel safe."

"I'll have a look at it."

Sanderson thanks him. Should he stay, in case the man has any questions? Maybe he'd better not. He'd have no answers. "I'll be in the kitchen if you need me," he says. "Next door."

Dexter grunts and Sanderson retraces his steps to pull the front door to and dispose of his jacket. Noting that he hasn't made his bed, he straightens the bottom sheet, folds up his pyjamas and stuffs them under the pillow. As he passes the bathroom, Dexter is down on one knee. Like other tradesmen he must scorn comfort – why not use a cushion? Perhaps he is wearing kneepads. There is a bang and something hits the bottom of the bath. A rattle. The stopper?

If you need me, Sanderson had remarked. He pulls out a chair, tired all of a sudden. If you need me, give a shout. I'll be at your side before you can say Jack Robinson. Apprentice plumber at your service. I've reached the dark side of life, but a replacement lens will put that right. Once they get around to it, I'll be as good as new. No glaucoma in sight. I may lack knowledge and experience, but I'm willing to learn. So, if you need me…

The fact is no one does any longer.

Jackie, his daughter, did, at one time. Not in the early days – he would kiss her goodnight and that was it. Jean dealt with food, clothing and what have you. Nor did she seek him out in her teens. Ever independent, she went her own way. That changed with the arrival of the kids. With his wife gone, as often as not he was the one who took them out or picked them up from school. For a few years he'd been closer to his grandchildren than to his daughter. By and by, as was to be expected, they outgrew him. His youngest gave up on him the day she got her smartphone; at that point he hardly saw the others for their birthdays even. What could he give them from his world that belonged in theirs, except money?

"I'll take your picture, Grandpa," she offers and he looks up. She is standing in the doorway, across from him, a ten-year-old with a monster tattoo on her left arm and a ring in one ear. She has had it pierced. There is a flash and within seconds she shows him the result, his face warped, as in a funhouse mirror. Not that it's funny. She presses a key and other versions of him come and go, all equally distorted. "Now you're an ape," she tells him and there is truly a striking likeness. Half man, half monkey. He tries to laugh with her.

"How did you do that?" he asks.

"It's an app."

He takes her word for it.

Her features blur and her voice deepens. "I'll have to put in a new one," she says.

"An app?"

"What app? A bath shower mixer."

The girl is gone and where she stood there is a stranger. No, no stranger. Fletcher?

"It's shot to hell with corrosion," he mutters. "I've got one in the van. I won't be long. Better fill a jug. I have to switch the water off at the mains."

"At the mains," echoes Sanderson, but the man has vanished.

The main arteries carry blood away from the heart. The veins bring it back.

His last medical was fine. Whatever else ails him, there's no corrosion – though that wasn't the term the doctor used. Why can't they speak plain English?

Realizing he is on his own, Sanderson gets to his feet to check on Fletcher's progress. He takes in the scene. The bath mat is scrunched up in a corner and there are tools everywhere. Among them are some whose function he would be hard put to guess at. He stoops to pick up a gadget with handles, like pliers, and has to steady himself. Some sort of cutter, he assumes, but what precisely? The letters O, R, L must indicate different settings, some figures – 0, 45, 90, 135, 180 – likewise, but for what purpose? R must mean right, L left, but what could O stand for? And the figures? The angle, presumably, but of what? He loses himself in thought. Then, careful to bend his knees and not his back, he lets the tool slide out of his hand and on to the floor. He rights himself, clutching at the washbasin, in which a drill has found a temporary home. The size of the instrument is impressive – it could get through the wall into his neighbour's flat in an instant. And what would she do? Most likely plug up her end and use it as a peephole. Nosy bugger. He would give her something to gawk at. In a sudden spurt of anger, he flushes the toilet. There is still water in the cistern.

"You'll have to excuse the mess." Fletcher has reappeared and clears part of the floor with his foot in order to dump the box he is carrying. "I'm usually tidy, but at the moment nothing's going my way." He pats his pockets and brings out a set of keys. "These must be yours. They were in the door."

Sanderson, about to ease past him, accepts the keys. It's not the first time he has left them in the door, but Fletcher needn't be apprised of the fact.

"Would you like a cup of tea?" he asks. "Or coffee? My daughter prefers coffee."

"There's no water," he is told. "Unless you filled a pot? No? Thanks anyway."

In the kitchen he tries the tap. Fletcher is right. He catches sight of the dispenser for his pills, open at Thursday, and knits his eyebrows in an attempt to determine whether or not he took his tablets this morning. Is today Thursday or Friday? Not Saturday, or else Fletcher wouldn't be there. He'd better find out.

The area behind the bath is almost bare; the taps are gone as is the shower. The bathroom is no longer his.

"Excuse me," he says. "You wouldn't happen to know what day it is?"

"Friday," Fletcher informs him. "The twentieth. It's the spring equinox."

He knew that. "Did you see it?" he asks.

"See what?"

"The equinox."

Fletcher gives him a quick glance. "The eclipse, you mean. Well, there wasn't much to see, was there? The sky was overcast. It got a bit darker, was all."

"Yes." Sanderson hadn't noticed it getting darker, but his windows face north and west and what there was of twilight must have been over by the time he got himself outside. He'd mistaken the hour. "They say there'll be another in 2090," he points out.

"I'll make a note of it." Fletcher rips the box open and pulls out a showerhead on a hose. He puts it aside and rummages through the rest of the parts.

"If there's anything you want…"

232

There is no reply so Sanderson retreats to the kitchen.

Funny how he can keep numbers in mind so much more easily than names or words. There'll be one in 2090, he had said, without hesitating. He may try and use the main door code downstairs to access his bank account, or vice versa, but at least he gets the sequence right. Names come and go, like transient visitors. Fletcher had given his name only an hour ago and already Sanderson is uncertain: was it indeed Fletcher? Wasn't it Spencer? The problem has been with him for years. Jackie, in naming her three girls, had begged for trouble: Ellie, Millie and Emily, pleasant enough on their own, form a veritable trap. For a while he made a joke of it, grasping at whatever name surfaced – and who might you be? Susan? Sarah? Sally? – and had them correct him, but they soon tired of his stratagem. He would have bought them T-shirts with their names, ideally on both sides, if they had been available. It is no consolation that the void is temporary: the name or word that he is after will pop up unexpectedly out of nowhere, but once that occurs there is no one, nothing, there to hang it on. The doorway is empty.

He walks through it. On the living room wall, across from the bathroom, are photos of his wife, Jackie and the girls. Jean's has faded, as has his memory of her: she will remain forever mini-skirted, in her mid-twenties, and not the person he lived with for so many years. Jackie must have been sixteen or so when hers was taken, the children approximately ten, eight, and four. They have naturally changed a lot. If he were to hand someone these pictures and have them identify the four in a line-up, they would fail miserably. Actually, what he should do is leave Jean's where it is but remove the other two and put up one of Jackie when she was her mother's age. In years to come, rather than a group portrait, he could have one of each of his grandchildren as they reach twenty-five. Five twenty-

233

five-year-olds – the symmetry appeals to him. There would certainly be marked differences between them but also similarities, like with the petals of a flower. Should he have them form a circle, like a buttercup?

He is interrupted in his musings by the sound of a drill, gradually increasing in volume. Fletcher must be about to install what was in the box. Suddenly there is the crunch of metal hitting something hard, followed by a string of expletives. Some obstacle has blocked his progress. His neighbour? But how?

"What's up?" he asks, edging towards the bathroom.

Fletcher's shoulders sag.

"The bloody bit snapped. Like I said, this is not my day."

"Are you going to pack it in?"

Fletcher's eyebrows go up; the drill that let him down droops at his side. "And leave it like this? Wash my hands of it?" He gestures at the wall, completely bare, at the floor, anything but. The box, emptied, has found refuge in the bath.

"You're right." Sanderson backs out. He shuts the door to the living room. If he were on his own, he would make himself comfortable in one of the armchairs and close his eyes for a catnap, but with Fletcher around he can't. It's not that he doesn't trust the man, but... well, he doesn't, does he? What would have happened if he hadn't arrived home as he did? He might have found the flat stripped of everything of value. A hard chair will ensure that he keeps alert.

About to sit down, he spots the pill dispenser. Friday's tablets call for his attention. On the side is an empty glass, left in readiness. He turns on the tap – or tries to – and remembers that the water is off at the mains. His door unlocked, the water cut off, the drill bit breaking in two – nothing is as it should be.

But why blame his neighbour – or Fletcher? It must have been wear and tear that made the bit snap. If planes crash without warning, why not a bit? The problem is so common that it even has a name. He casts around for it, glass in hand, but nothing comes up. With the names of people, he sometimes goes through the alphabet, pausing after each letter in the hope that one of them will hook another, but with words generally this tactic has never proved successful. Fletcher could probably tell him. He seems to know his job.

As if to underline the man's competence, the drill starts up, the sound rising in pitch and volume. Once it has reached a certain level it remains there – until it drops quickly and dies away. The sequence is repeated at short intervals. What follows is a series of clanking noises. Fletcher must be assembling what was in the box.

Putting the empty glass down, Sanderson sees before him another box, one a lot smaller. He fingers the primitive screwdriver in his hand, made out of a twisted piece of grey metal, shaped like a question mark, and visualizes the perforated strips and plates, red and green, that served to construct lorries, cranes and planes. Wheels. Axles. Was there also a booklet with instructions? He can't recall. There were the little square nuts. There was the miniature spanner. There were bolts of various length. And where did it end up? He should have asked his brother while he was around. He should have asked his parents. Now no one has the answer. Not that it makes any difference. He wasn't very good at mechanics as a child and these days simply winding a watch would be a struggle – if they sold watches that had to be wound.

He wonders if Fletcher had a set as a boy. Was that what made him choose his line of work?

Checking in on him, he finds him busy, about to fasten

235

a vertical rod alongside the two pipes that run from the ceiling down to a heavy-looking contraption above the bath. Blinded by the reflection off the chrome fittings, Sanderson screws up his eyes. He clears his throat.

Fletcher stiffens. "Yes?"

"Would you like me to hold it for you?"

Fletcher vacillates.

"There's no room," he says eventually. "We'd get in each other's way."

"I used to be fairly good with my hands," Sanderson assures him. It is a weak protest. "I had a Meccano set as a boy."

"Mhm."

"Did you?"

"Did I what?"

"Did you have one?"

"No. Why?"

"I just wondered. I built all sorts of things and took them apart again." He doesn't have to let on that they rarely matched his expectations.

"Well, I wouldn't want you to try that here."

The rod is in place, with a holder for the showerhead. Fletcher hooks a soap dish onto it and finally the showerhead itself. "That's it," he says. "Done."

He tilts his head, clearly proud of his work.

"It's very different." Sanderson is apprehensive. With the glare from the metal in his eyes, he can make out no handle or knob with which to get the water running, none to regulate the temperature, none to redirect the stream from bath to shower. Not that that matters particularly – a bath strikes him as safer. But how fill it? He approaches it for a closer look. "What was wrong with the old one?"

"This is the kind we're installing today. It's more economical. Besides, people want change."

"I don't."

"You have to move with the times."

Sanderson doesn't agree, but what would be the point in arguing? Fletcher is merely following orders. "How does it work?" he asks.

Fletcher instructs him. "Two knobs," he says, indicating first one side of the tap, then the other. "One to control the flow: On. Off. The other the temperature: Hot. Cold." He grasps one of them and moves it around. "On. Off." He steps aside. "You try it."

Sanderson does. The knob, which blends into the structure so well he'd been unable to detect it initially, is hard to grip; no water comes. Of course – it's off at the mains.

"Feel the rubbery ridge?" Fletcher's eyes meet his. "There's a lock. If you press down on the ridge and go on turning, the water will run faster. The same with the other knob. It goes from cold to hot in a jiffy. Got it?"

"I'm not sure. What's this thing in the middle?"

"That's to change from bath to shower. You have to have the water running for it to work."

Sanderson pushes down on the knob, but it has to be pulled up. Nothing happens.

"I see," he says, without conviction. "Is there a manual?"

Fletcher shakes his head. "But you'll soon get the hang of it. Nothing can go wrong, really. The locks are there to make it childproof."

Is that what this is about? With an ageing population, will the taps everywhere have to be replaced? Will they bar the windows too, to stop him from falling out? "That's comforting," he tells Fletcher, but the man isn't tuned in to irony.

"I'll nip down to switch the water on again," he says.

And he disappears.

Sanderson stays in the bathroom and before long the water is on: the cistern of the toilet is filling up. He peers at the new device, but there is no trickle from either tap or showerhead.

"Did you try it?" Fletcher has returned. "No? I thought I heard water running as I came through the door."

Sanderson shakes his head. "That was from the toilet."

But the sound is still there, if faint. They both listen.

"The kitchen," says Fletcher.

"My tablets," says Sanderson. "I forgot…"

That night his back bothers him more than it has done for months. He will have to try and sleep without a pillow. Spector – the name had come to him in a flash – had helped him: with the dishcloth blocking the drain, the place had been flooded. Afterwards Spector had repeated his instructions and supervised him as he got the water running, set it at the right temperature and, taking a deep breath, shifted from bath to shower. He had scribbled ON/OFF and HOT/COLD on bits of the cardboard that had kept the mixer parts separate in the box and taped them to the wall, not easy to read, but the effort should count for something. "Phil," Sanderson had said on parting, assuming a familiarity that didn't seem inappropriate, "I preferred it the way it was, but I suppose I'll get used to the new one in time. Thank you." Spector had hesitated, about to say something, but didn't. He just patted him on the shoulder, fastened the tool belt around his waist and left.

Now, in his dressing gown, Sanderson eyes the bath. Five minutes, and there would be enough water for a soak to ease his aching back. Five minutes. But that would be five minutes in which a lot could go wrong.

Burst arteries.

And along with that phrase, the term he had been searching for rises out of some recess in his brain: metal fatigue. That was it. Metal fatigue makes the wheels of trains crumble, the wings of planes disintegrate and drill bits snap. That was what he had wanted to mention to Spector. But no doubt Spector knows. He knew his job, at any rate.

Again, Sanderson studies the result. He wavers. There is of course a safe alternative. In the kitchen there is water. In the kitchen is a bucket. How many trips could it take?

He decides to go for the easy option.

About the author
L. F. Roth has had stories published in competition anthologies brought out by Biscuit Publishing, Earlyworks Press, Bridge House Publishing, Cinnamon Press, AudioArcadia.com, Momaya Press, University of Huddersfield Press, The Plymouth Writers Group and Black Pear Press. They generally focus on relationships, gender issues and trauma – at times all three. For details and a few excerpts, see
https://sites.google.com/site/lfroth1/

Index of Authors

Sally Angell, 54
Christopher Bowles, 69
M Bulleyment, 30
Elizabeth Cox, 90
Stephen Faulkner, 16
Alyson Faye, 8
Linda Flynn, 127
Boris Glikman, 185
Ian Inglis, 150
Karen Kendrick, 138
Dawn Knox, 190
Stuart Larner, 182
G. Norman Lippert, 116
Kay Middlemiss, 64
Adrian Naylor, 97
Jennie E. Owen, 26
Paula R C Readman, 207
L F Roth, 228
Michele Sheldon, 160
Dianne Stadhams, 132
Steve Wade, 170
Merlin Ward, 84
Clare Weze, 220
Anne Wilson, 46

Other Publications by Bridge House

Keepsake

by Jenny Palmer

Keepsake and Other Stories is an anthology of short stories by one of the growing number of brave women writers. Jenny Palmer brings us stories of otherness, witchcraft and magic close to home and further afield within Europe. We meet all sorts of characters: those who rely on guard dogs, those who shun social media and those who are obsessed. We even meet a Neanderthal man. There are paranormal stories, a story of bad neighbours, and a story of redundancy. And many more. All to be enjoyed.

"Jenny is totally in control of her stories. They are memorable and perfectly crafted." (*Amazon*)

Order from Amazon:

Paperback: ISBN 978-1-907335-57-0
eBook: ISBN 978-1-907335-58-7

Our Daily Bread

by Gill James

Our Daily Bread includes stories of people striving to succeed, sometimes managing, sometimes not. It is at the same time about daily lives and the bigger picture. There's the story of the young woman who struggles to come to terms with the death of her baby. A music manager is near to despair but finds a way to carry on. An older citizen finds that miracles still do happen. Even God, whoever she may be, has her say and gives us an interpretation of the Lord's Prayer.

Order from Amazon:

eBook: ASN B07GK1DGP4

Extraordinary

by Dawn Knox

From the furthest reaches of the universe, to the inside of a
cardboard box, assorted characters play deadly games with
their victims while others play practical jokes on angels or
dirty tricks on aliens. Some have good intentions, others are
scoundrels and a few are truly evil – but all of them are
EXTRAORDINARY.

"A wonderful collection of amazing stories. An enjoyable
read." (*Amazon*)

Order from Amazon:

Paperback: ISBN 978-1-907335-51-8
eBook: ISBN 978-1-907335-52-5

To Be... to Become

by Gill James

To Be... To Become is the theme of the 2018 Waterloo Festival Writing Competition. It is also the title of the e-book, which contains the sixteen winning entries. Some fantastic writing was offered and all of it was potentially publishable. We chose these because they told a good story, had a strong voice and were imaginative in their interpretation of the theme.

Entrants were asked to produce a short story or a monologue. Style was diverse and each story is completely different from the others.

Order from Amazon:

eBook: ISBN 978-1-907335-20-4